Pea, Bee, & Jay

STUCK TOGETHER

Brian "Smitty" Smith

An Im

D0956356

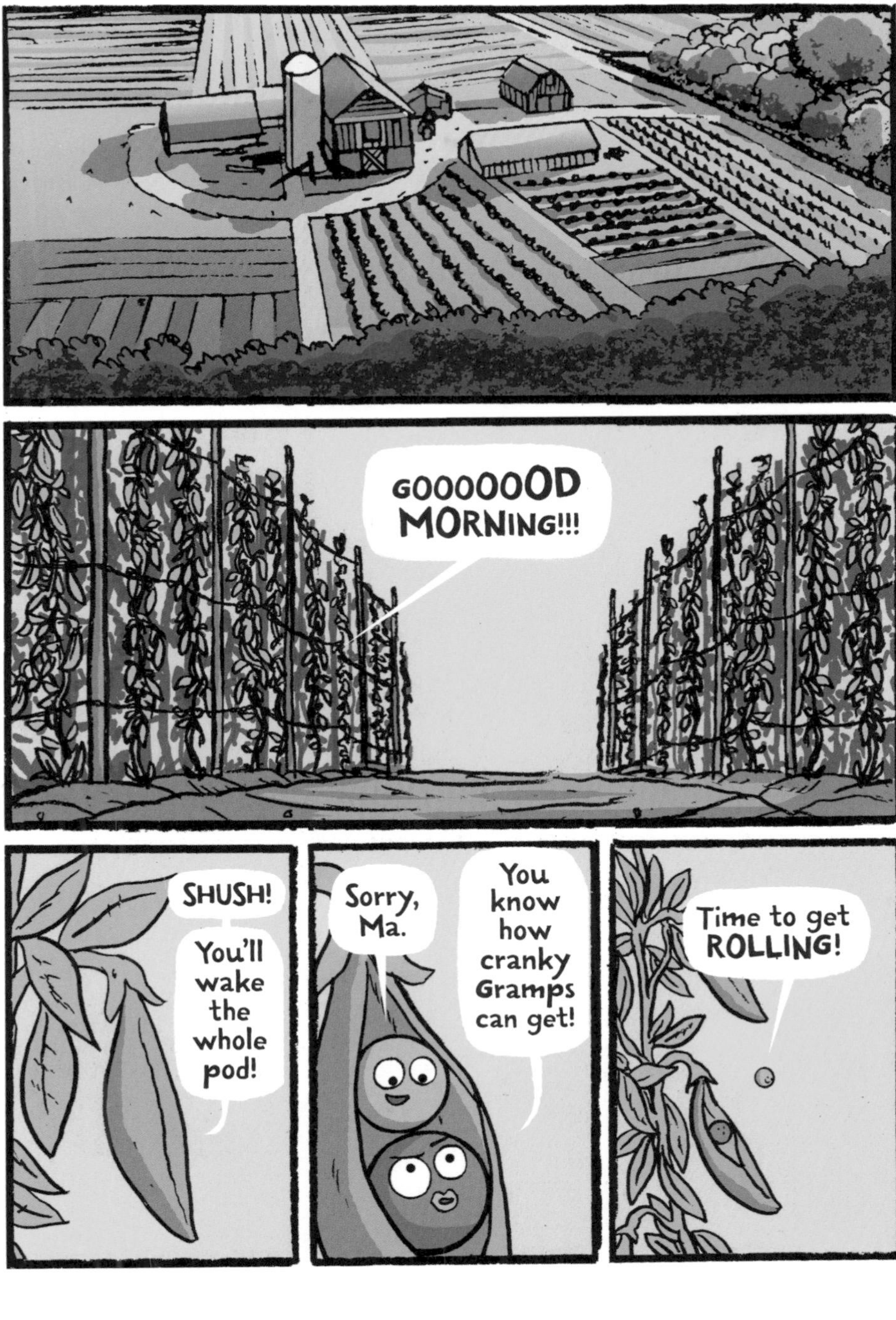
GOOOOOOD MORNING!!!
SHUSH!
You'll wake the whole pod!
Sorry, Ma.
You know how cranky Gramps can get!
Time to get ROLLING!

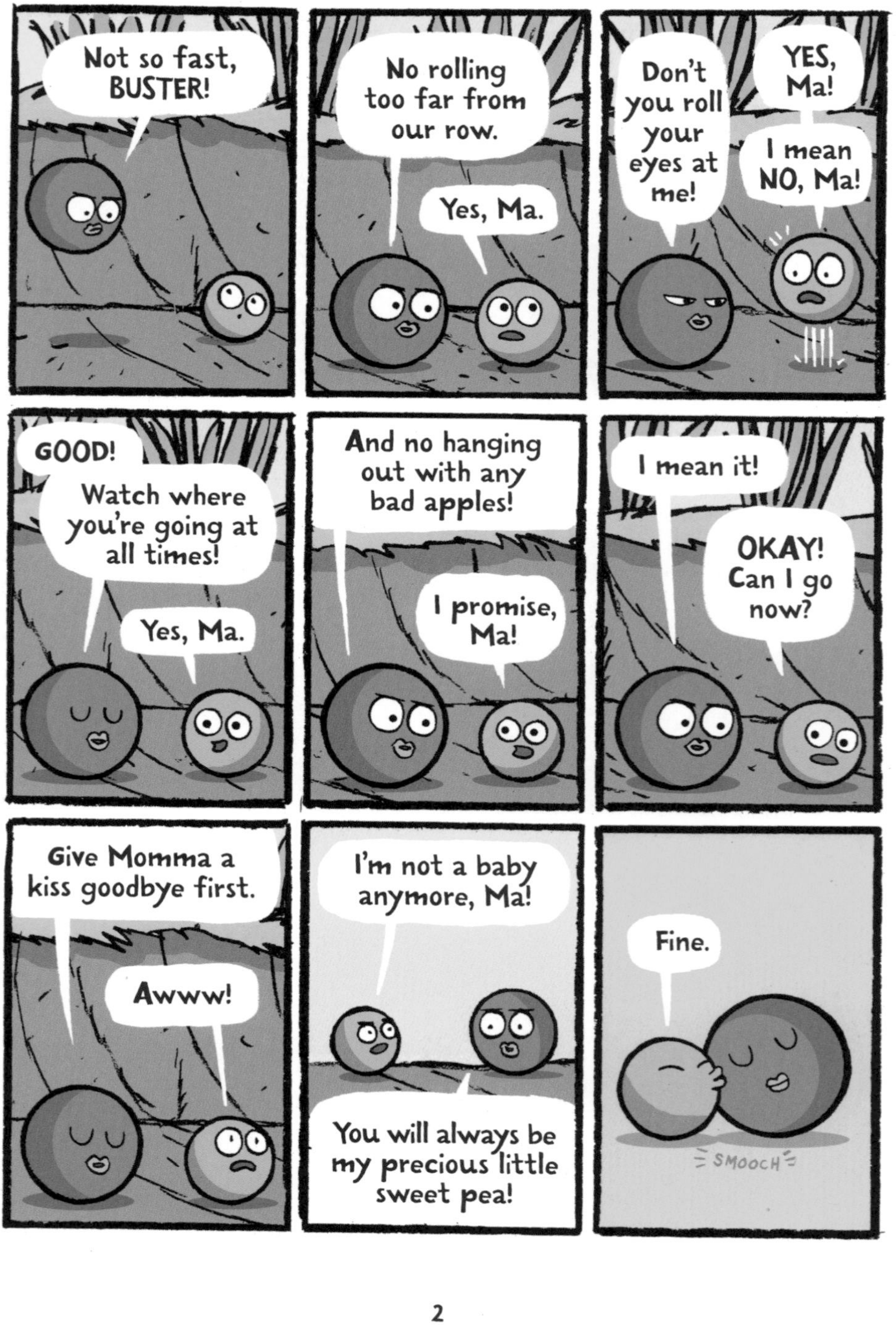
Not so fast, BUSTER!
No rolling too far from our row.
Yes, Ma.
Don't you roll your eyes at me!
YES, Ma!
I mean NO, Ma!
GOOD!
Watch where you're going at all times!
Yes, Ma.
And no hanging out with any bad apples!
I promise, Ma!
I mean it!
OKAY! Can I go now?
Give Momma a kiss goodbye first.
Awww!
I'm not a baby anymore, Ma!
You will always be my precious little sweet pea!
Fine.
SMOOCH

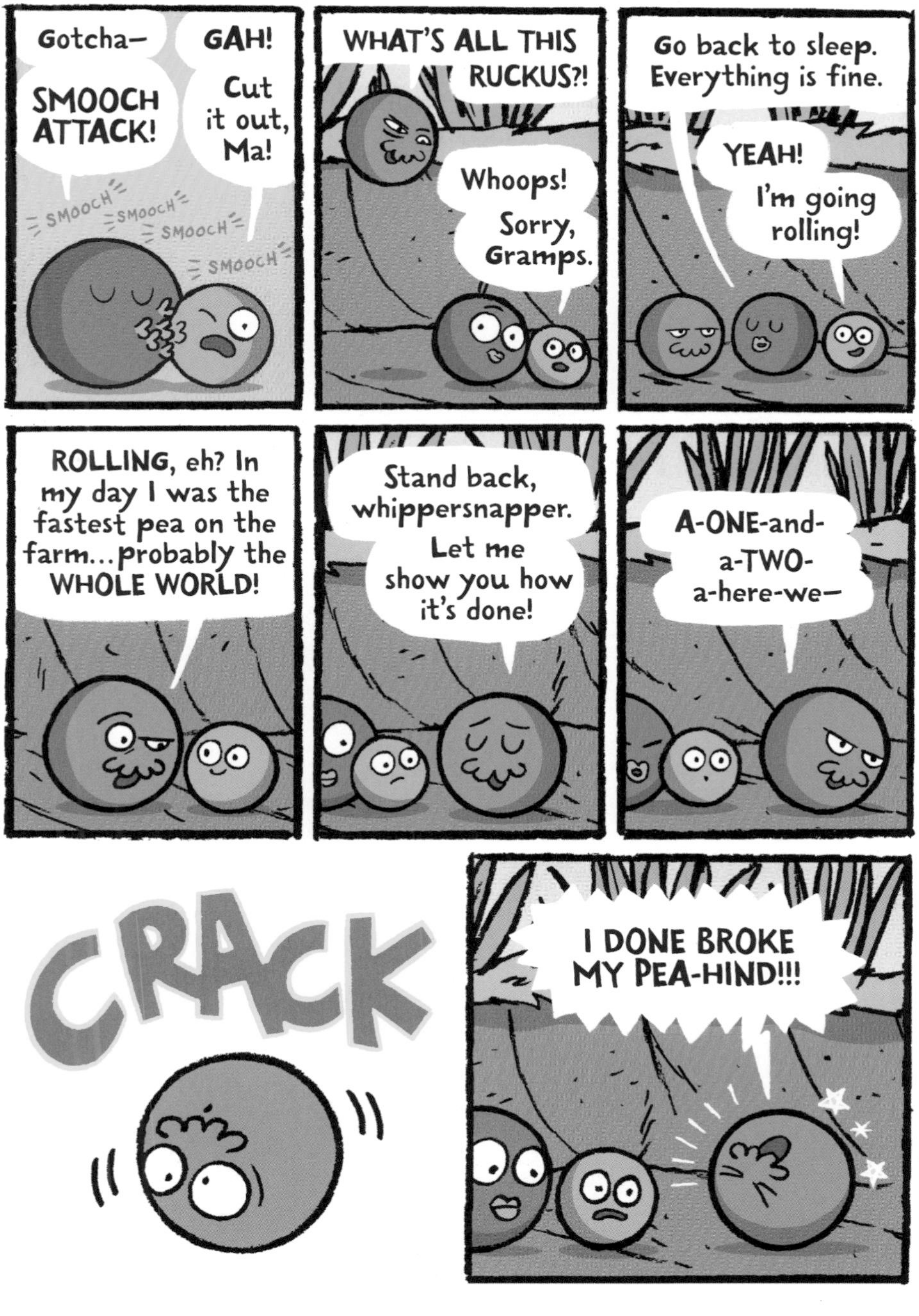
Gotcha—
SMOOCH ATTACK!
GAH!
Cut it out, Ma!
SMOOCH
SMOOCH
SMOOCH
SMOOCH
WHAT'S ALL THIS RUCKUS?!
Whoops!
Sorry, Gramps.
Go back to sleep. Everything is fine.
YEAH!
I'm going rolling!
ROLLING, eh? In my day I was the fastest pea on the farm...probably the WHOLE WORLD!
Stand back, whippersnapper.
Let me show you how it's done!
A-ONE-and-a-TWO-a-here-we—
CRACK
I DONE BROKE MY PEA-HIND!!!

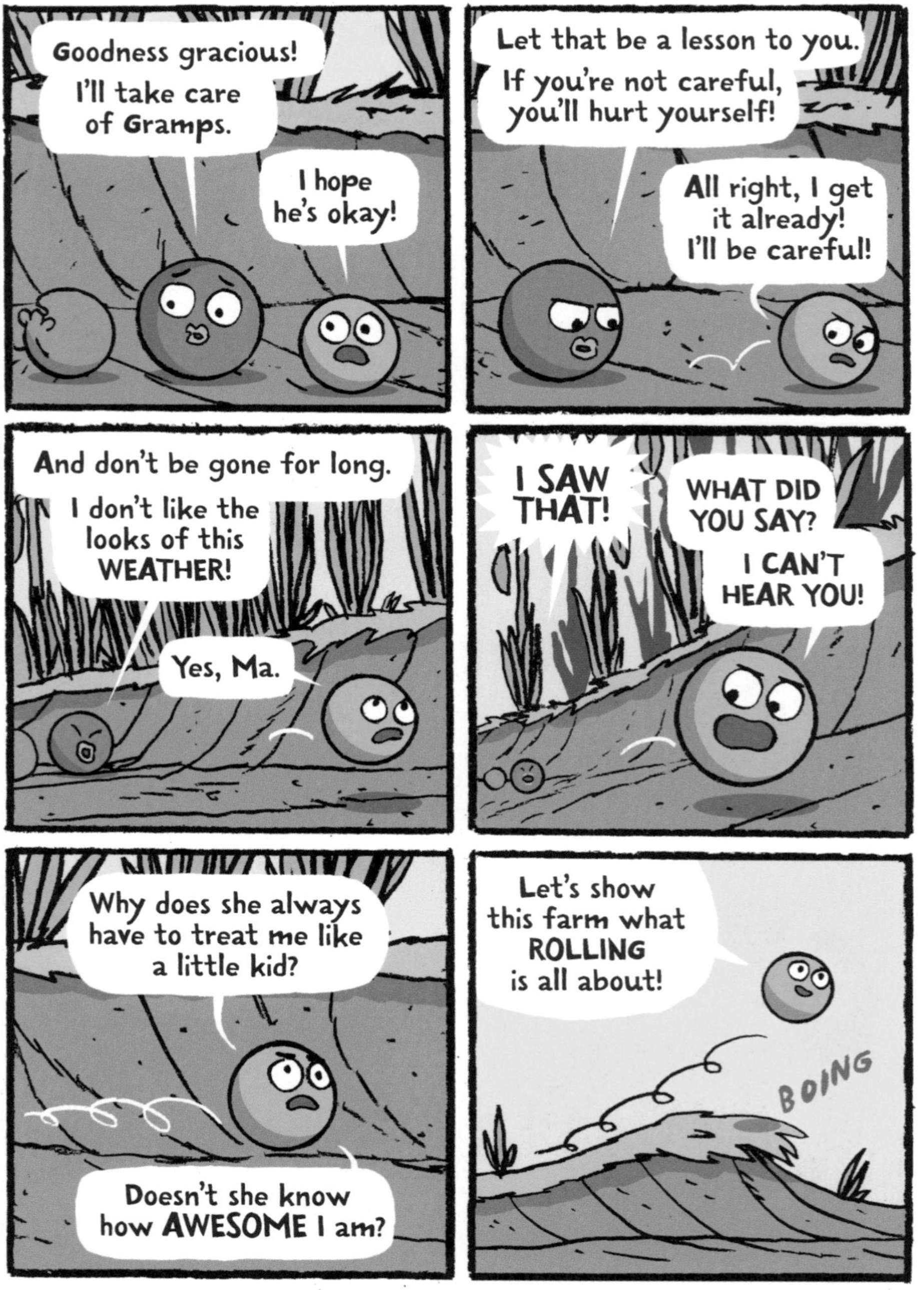
Goodness gracious!
I'll take care of Gramps.
I hope he's okay!
Let that be a lesson to you.
If you're not careful, you'll hurt yourself!
All right, I get it already! I'll be careful!
And don't be gone for long.
I don't like the looks of this WEATHER!
Yes, Ma.
I SAW THAT!
WHAT DID YOU SAY?
I CAN'T HEAR YOU!
Why does she always have to treat me like a little kid?
Doesn't she know how AWESOME I am?
Let's show this farm what ROLLING is all about!
BOING

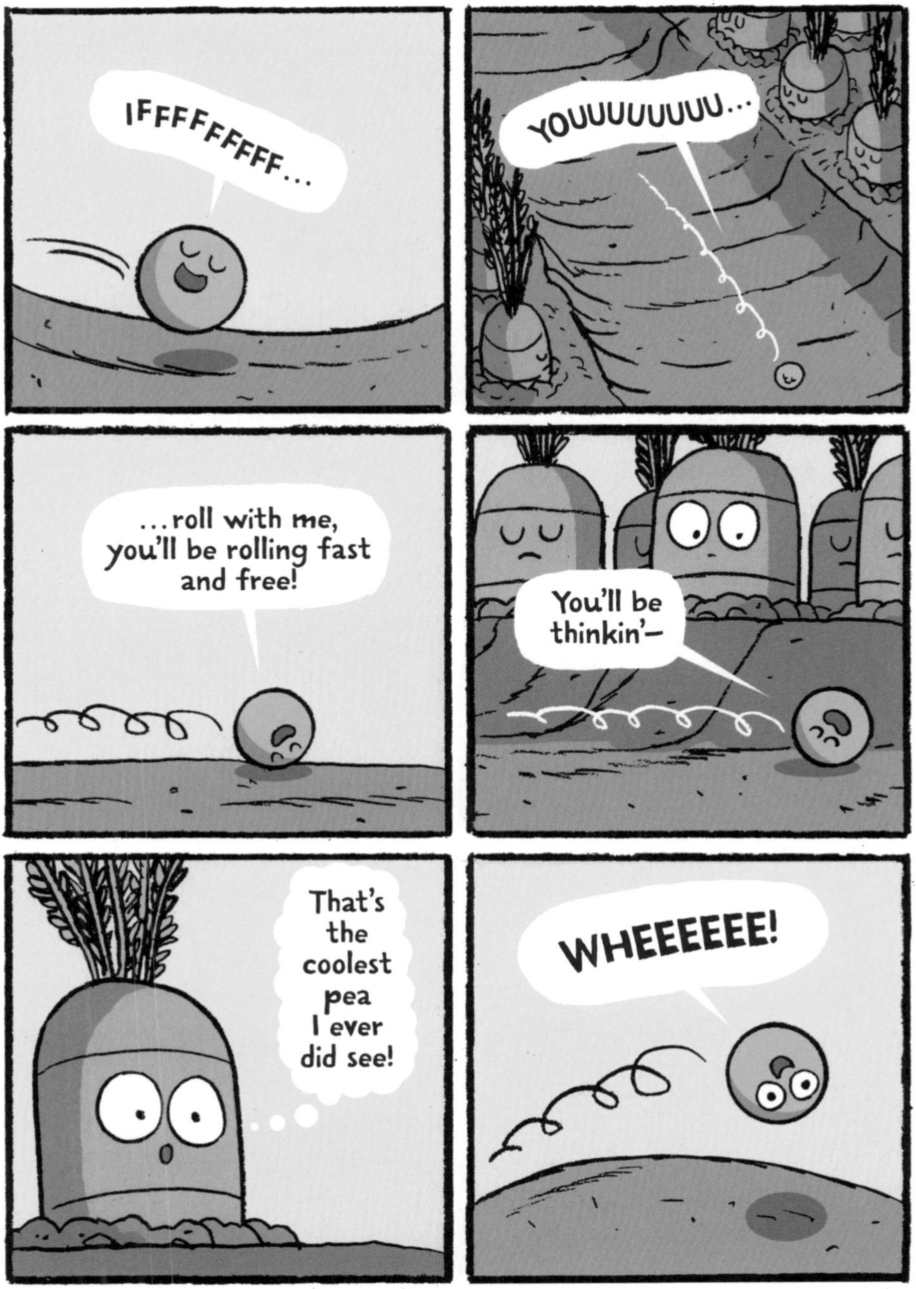
IFFFFFFFFF...
YOUUUUUUUU...
...roll with me, you'll be rolling fast and free!
You'll be thinkin'—
That's the coolest pea I ever did see!
WHEEEEEE!

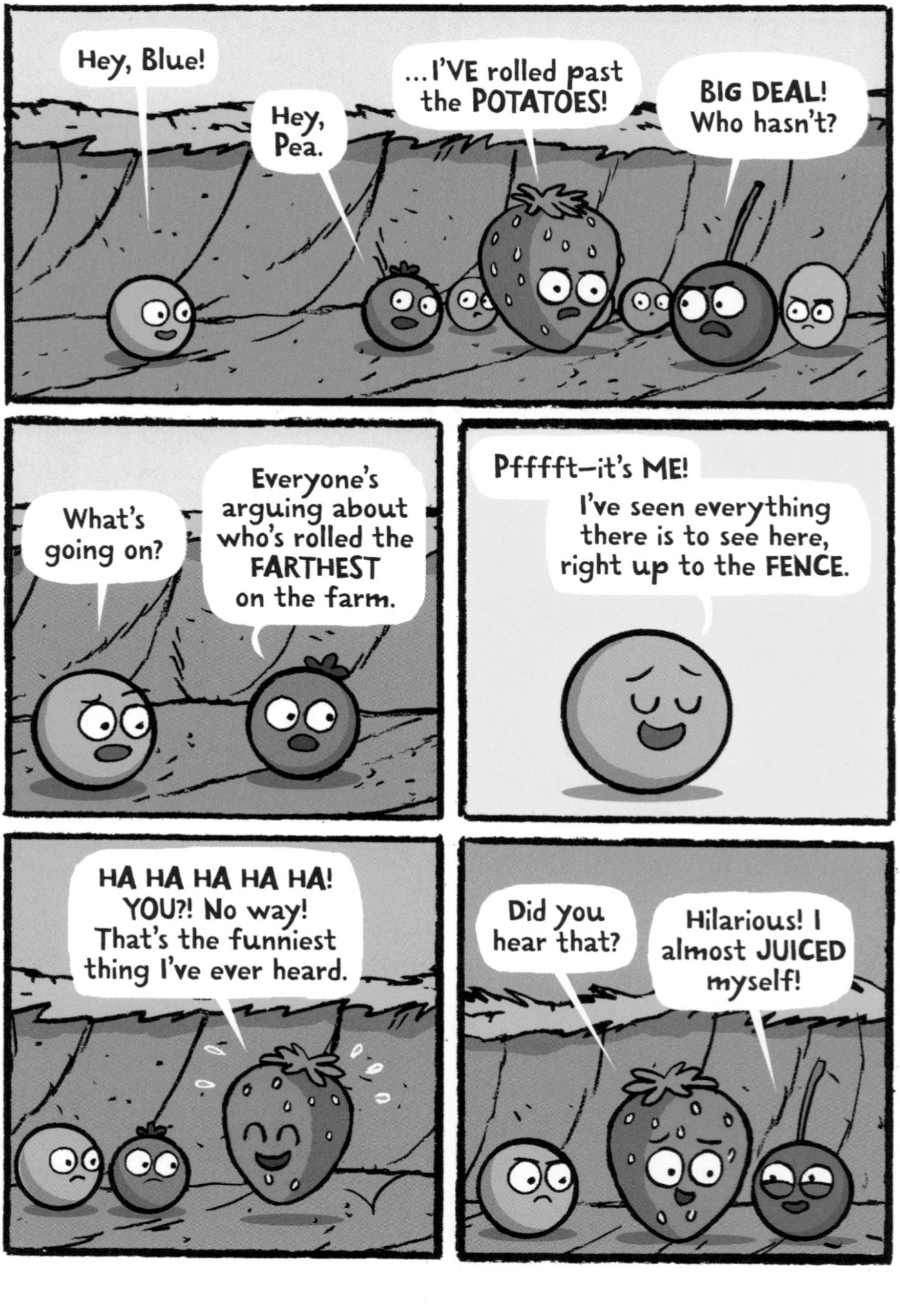
Hey, Blue!
Hey, Pea.
...I'VE rolled past the POTATOES!
BIG DEAL! Who hasn't?
What's going on?
Everyone's arguing about who's rolled the FARTHEST on the farm.
Pfffft—it's ME!
I've seen everything there is to see here, right up to the FENCE.
HA HA HA HA HA! YOU?! No way! That's the funniest thing I've ever heard.
Did you hear that?
Hilarious! I almost JUICED myself!

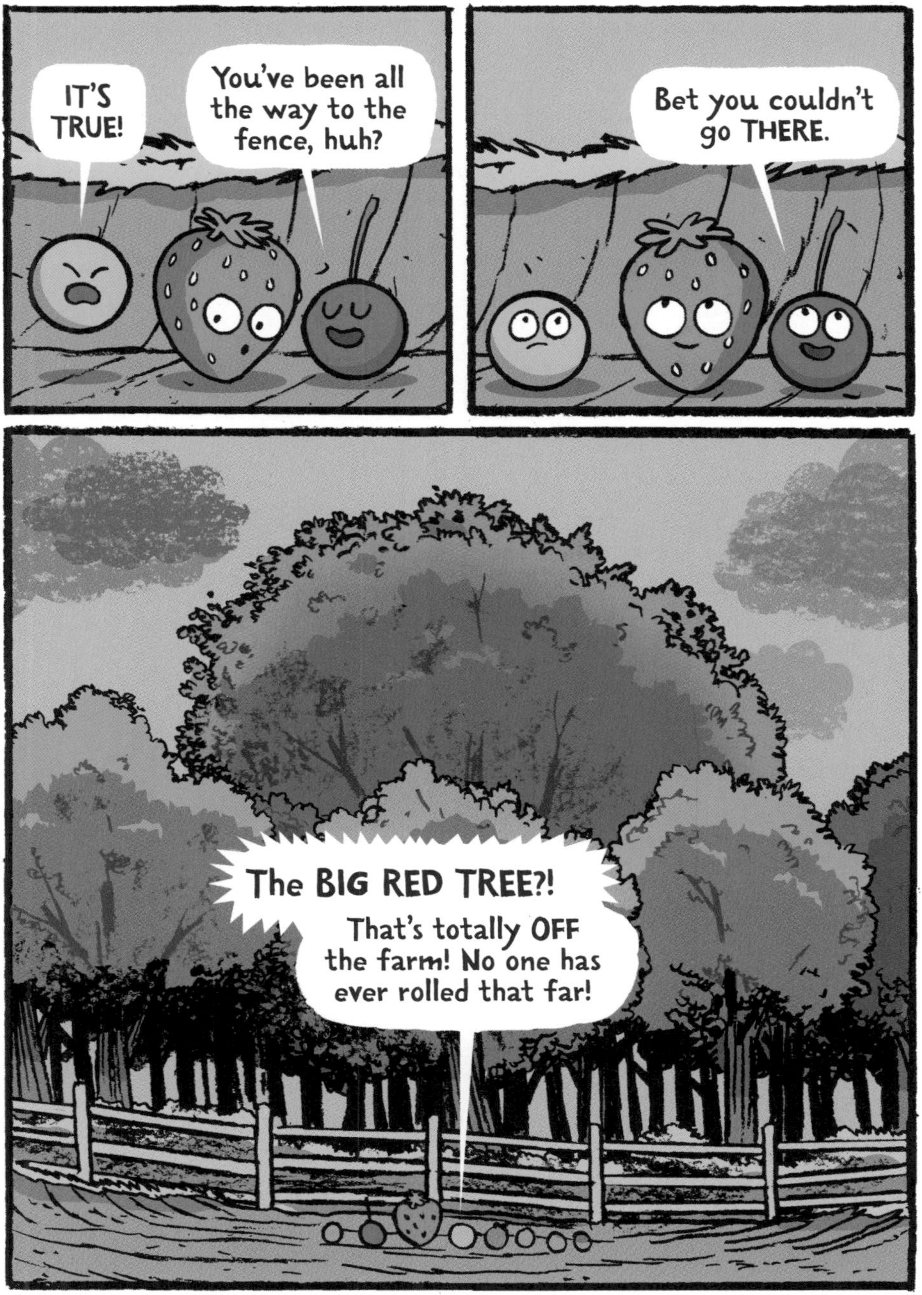
IT'S TRUE!
You've been all the way to the fence, huh?
Bet you couldn't go THERE.
The BIG RED TREE?!
That's totally OFF the farm! No one has ever rolled that far!

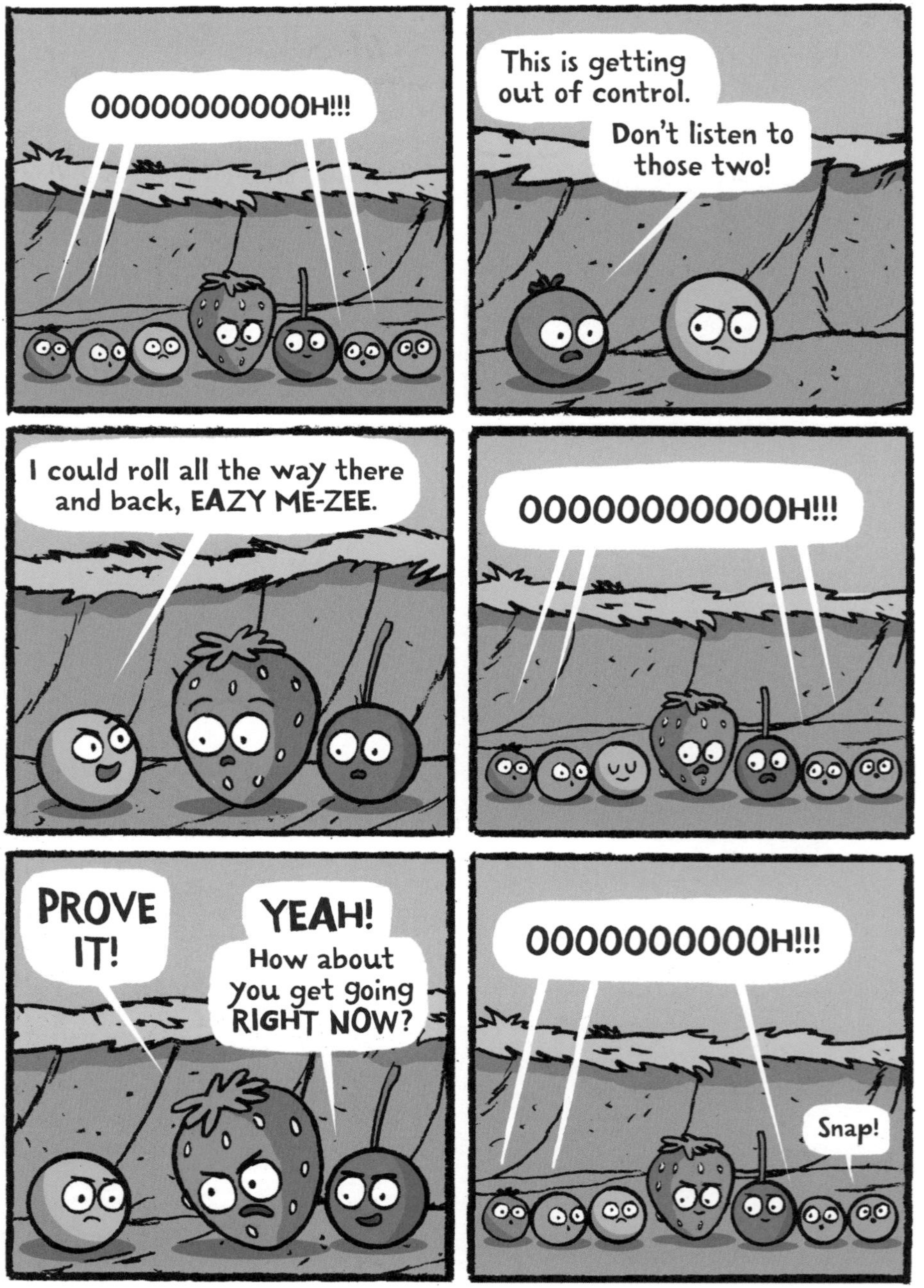
OOOOOOOOOOOH!!!
This is getting out of control.
Don't listen to those two!
I could roll all the way there and back, EAZY ME-ZEE.
OOOOOOOOOOOOH!!!
PROVE IT!
YEAH! How about you get going RIGHT NOW?
OOOOOOOOOOH!!!
Snap!

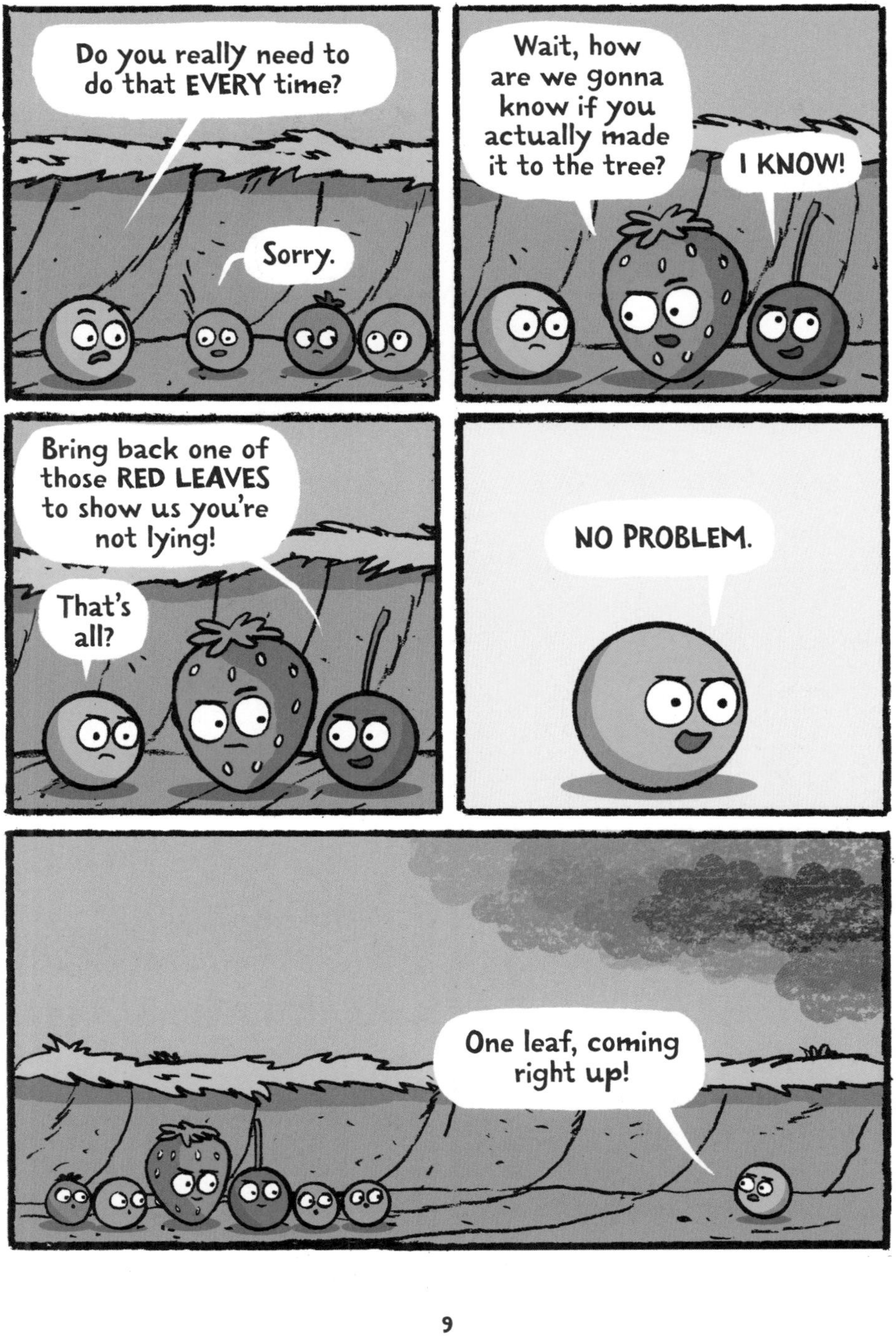
Do you really need to do that EVERY time?
Sorry.
Wait, how are we gonna know if you actually made it to the tree?
I KNOW!
Bring back one of those RED LEAVES to show us you're not lying!
That's all?
NO PROBLEM.
One leaf, coming right up!

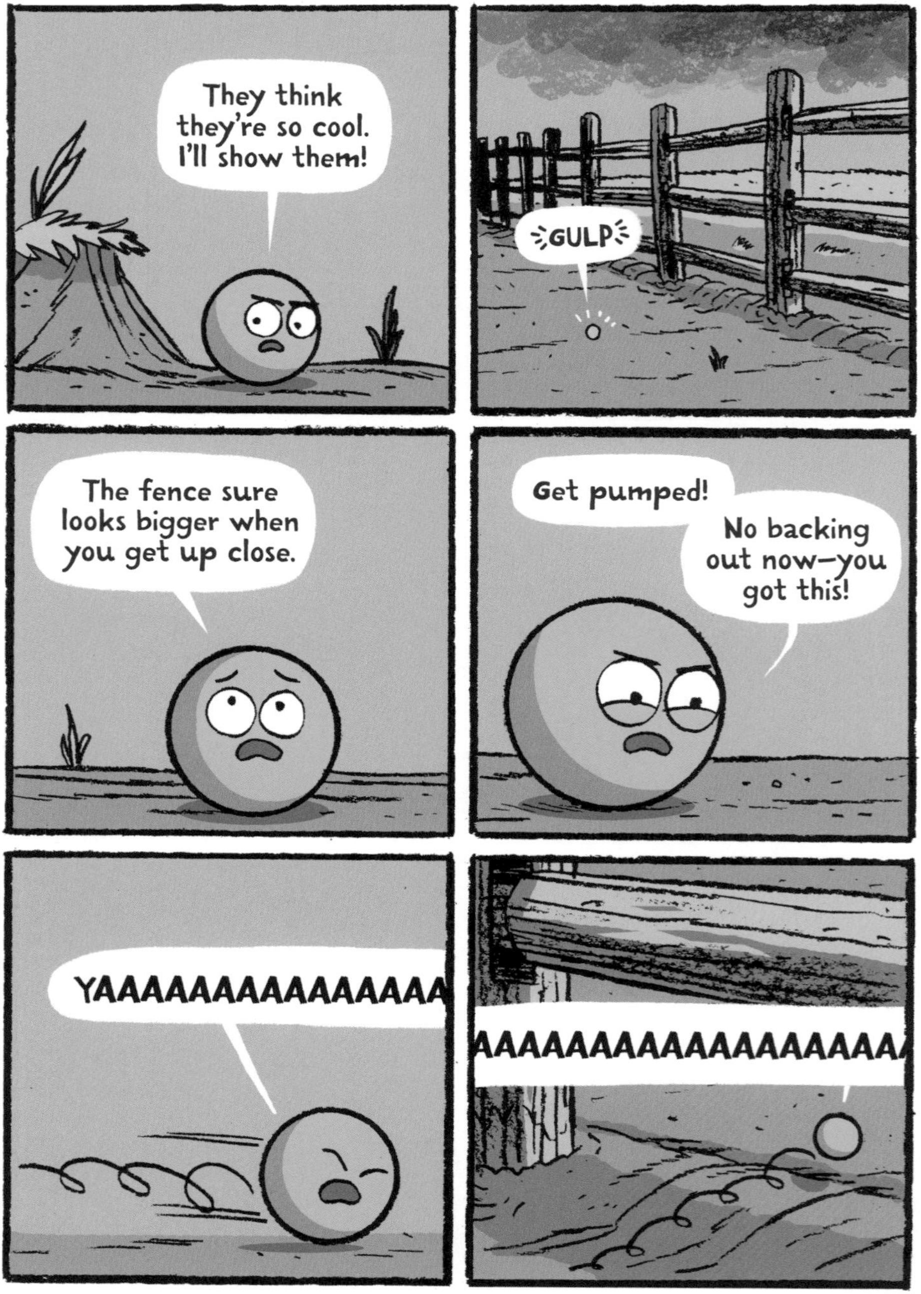

They think they're so cool. I'll show them!
GULP
The fence sure looks bigger when you get up close.
Get pumped!
No backing out now—you got this!
YAAAAAAAAAAAAAAAA
AAAAAAAAAAAAAAAAAAAAA

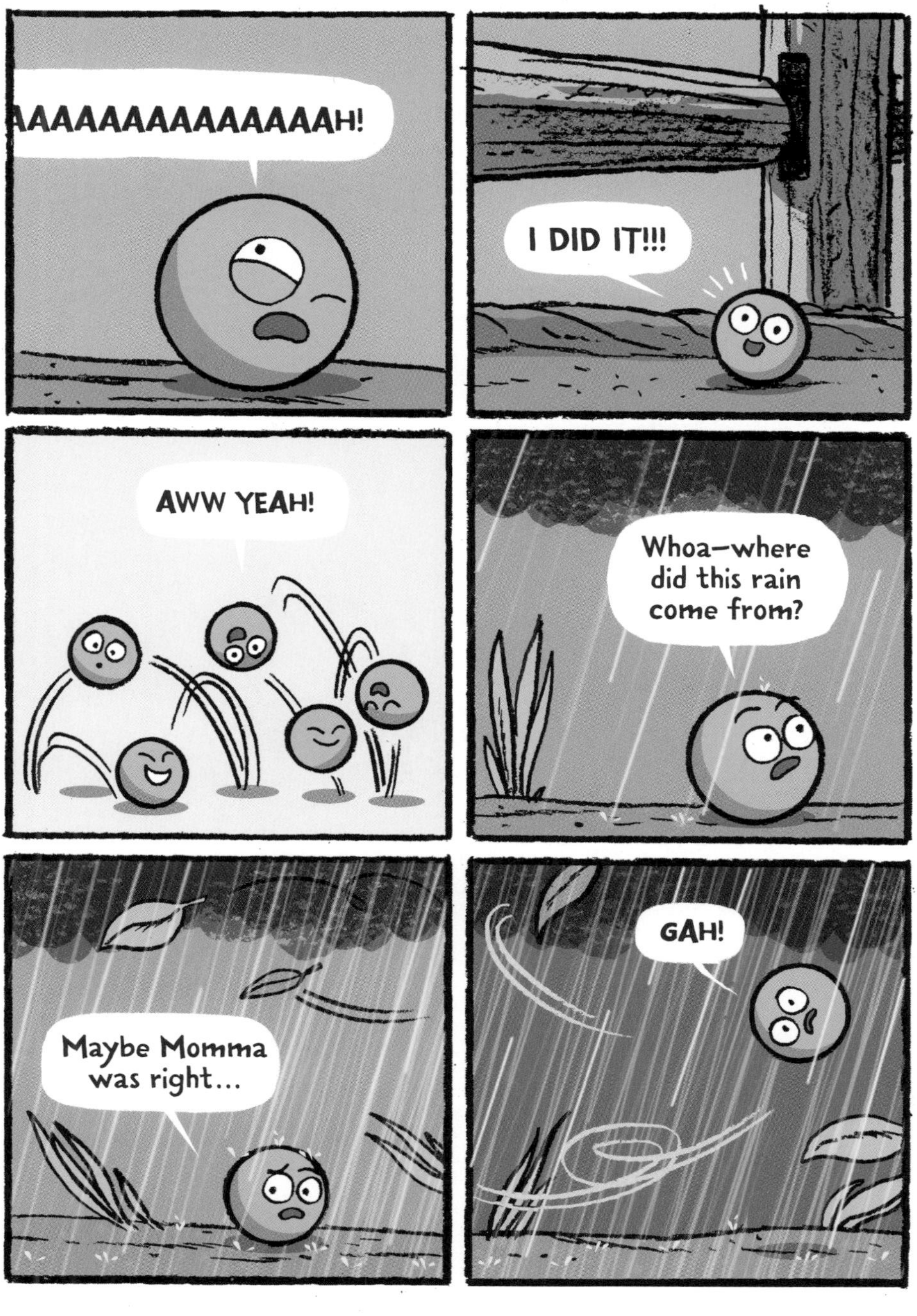
AAAAAAAAAAAAAAAH!
I DID IT!!!
AWW YEAH!
Whoa—where did this rain come from?
Maybe Momma was right...
GAH!

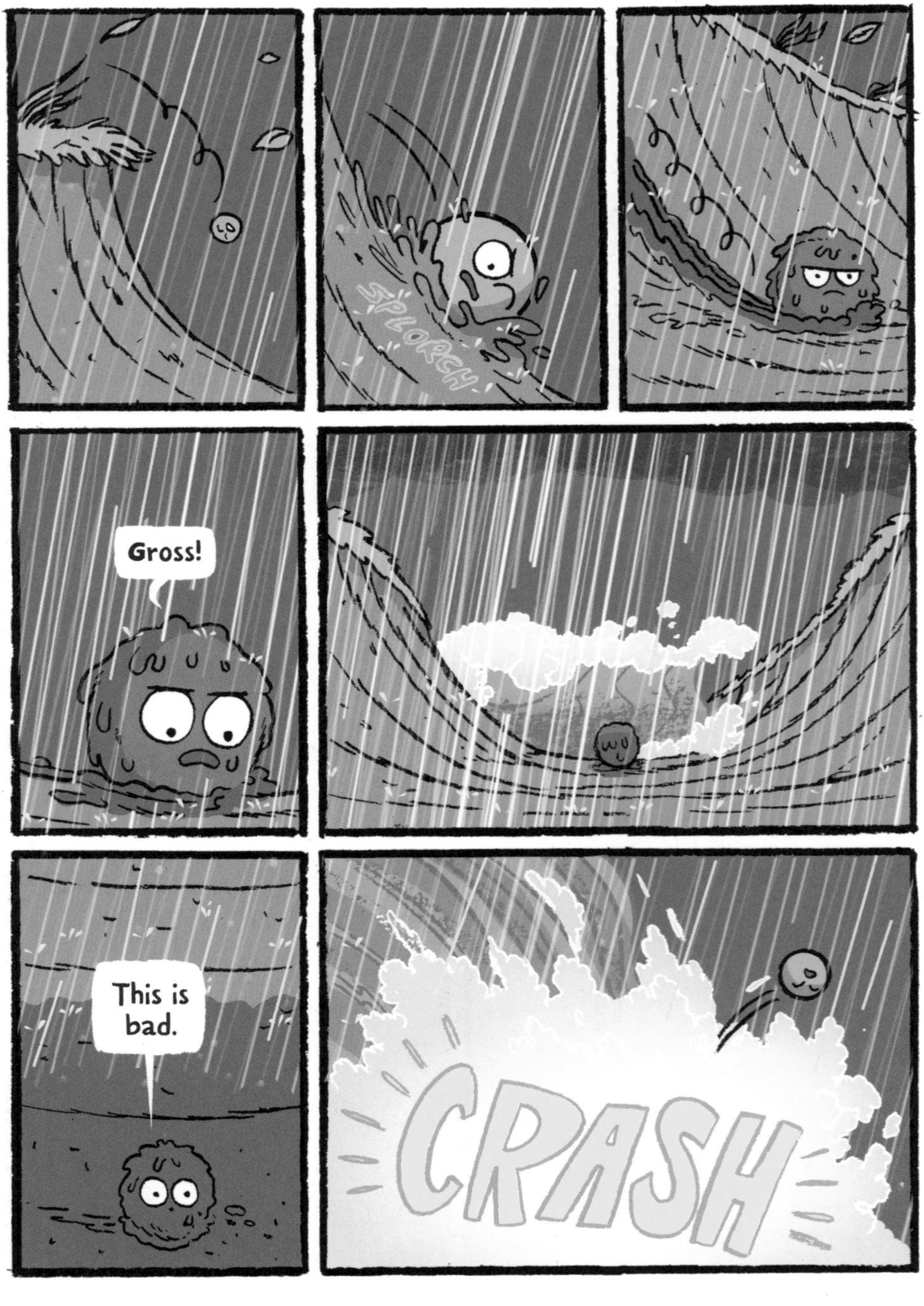
SPLORSH
Gross!
This is bad.
CRASH

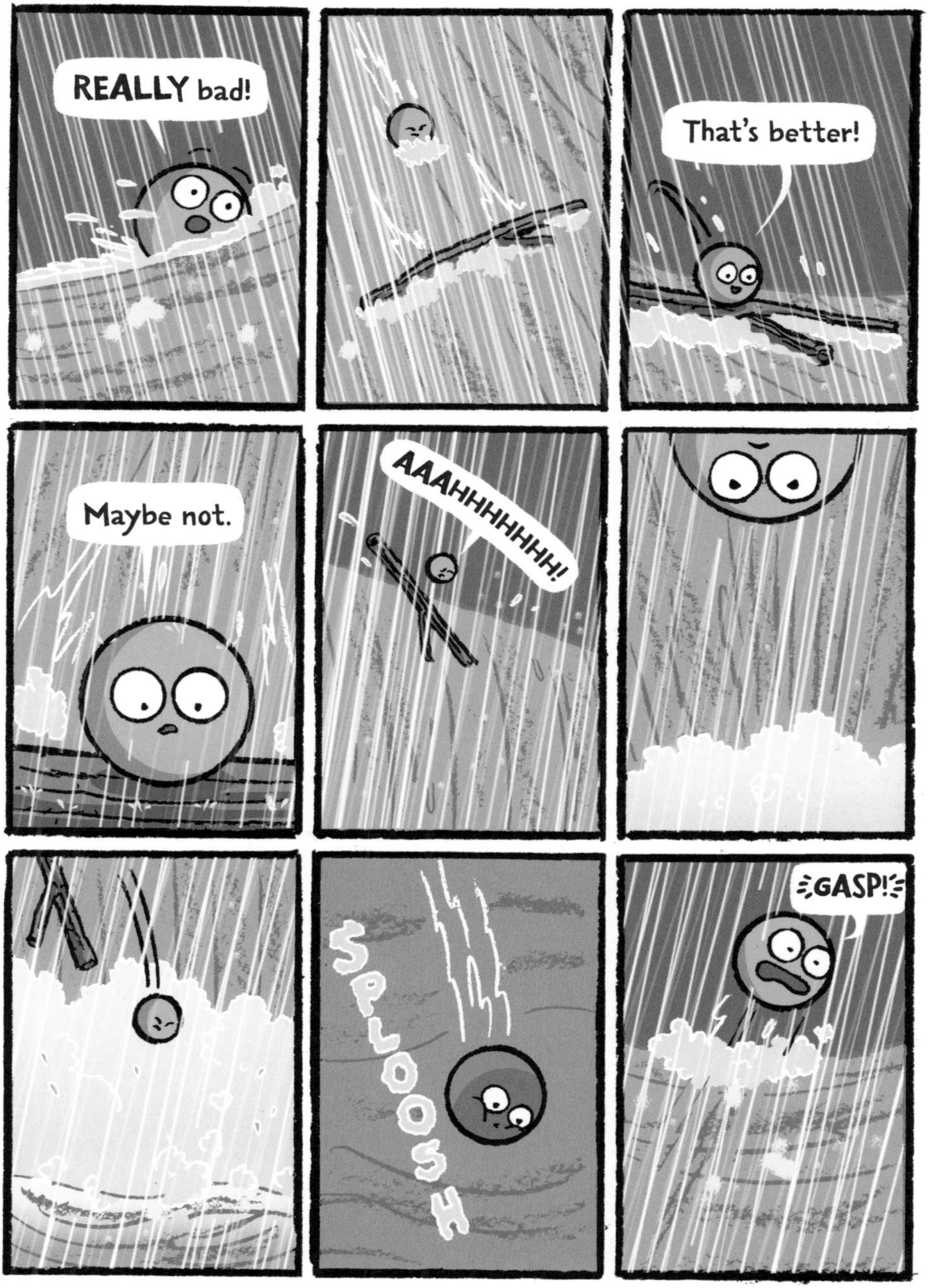
REALLY bad!
That's better!
Maybe not.
AAAHHHHHHHH!
SPLOOSH
GASP!

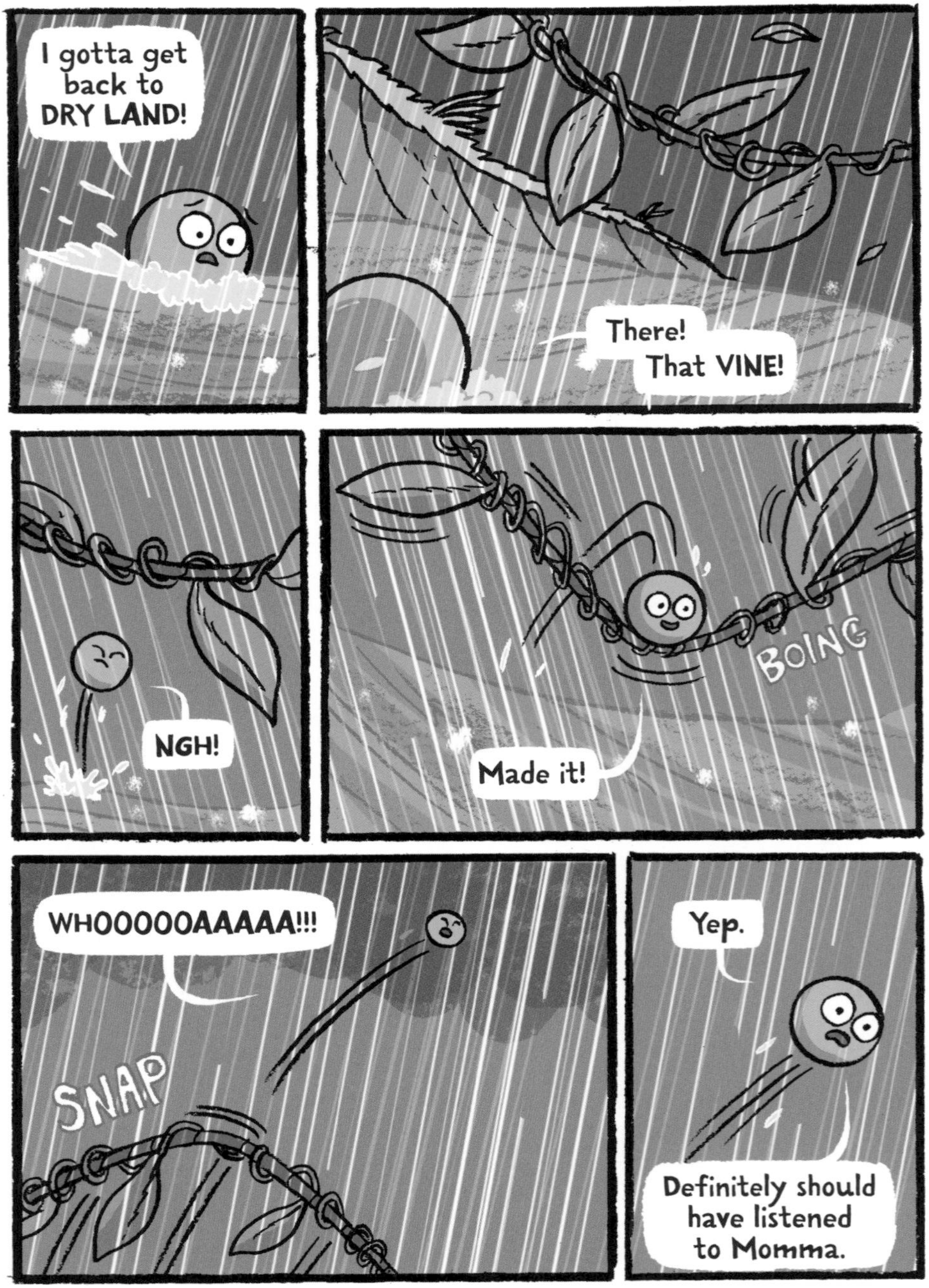
I gotta get back to DRY LAND!
There! That VINE!
NGH!
Made it!
BOING
WHOOOOOAAAAA!!!
SNAP
Yep.
Definitely should have listened to Momma.

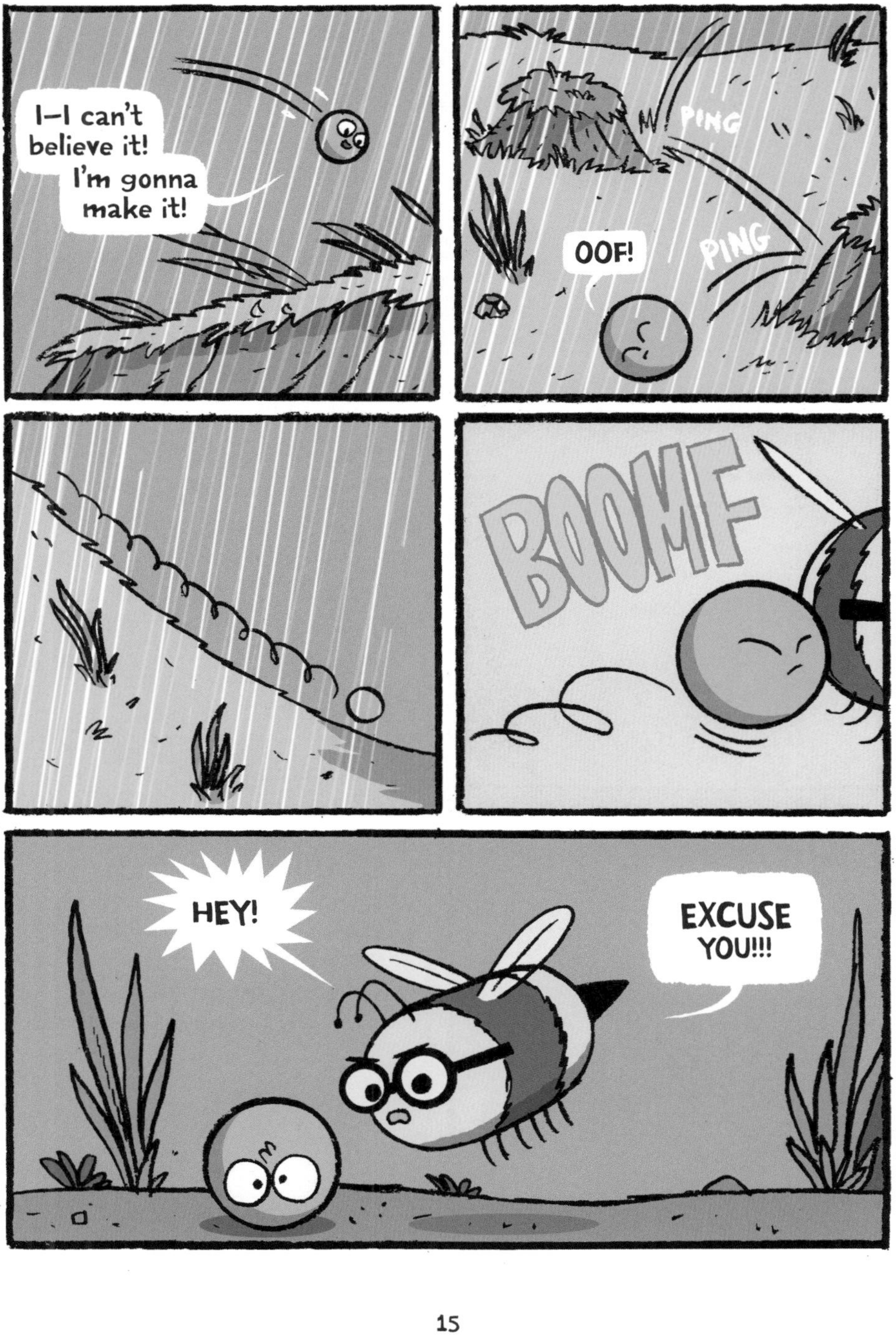
I-I can't believe it!
I'm gonna make it!
PING
PING
OOF!
BOOMF
HEY!
EXCUSE YOU!!!

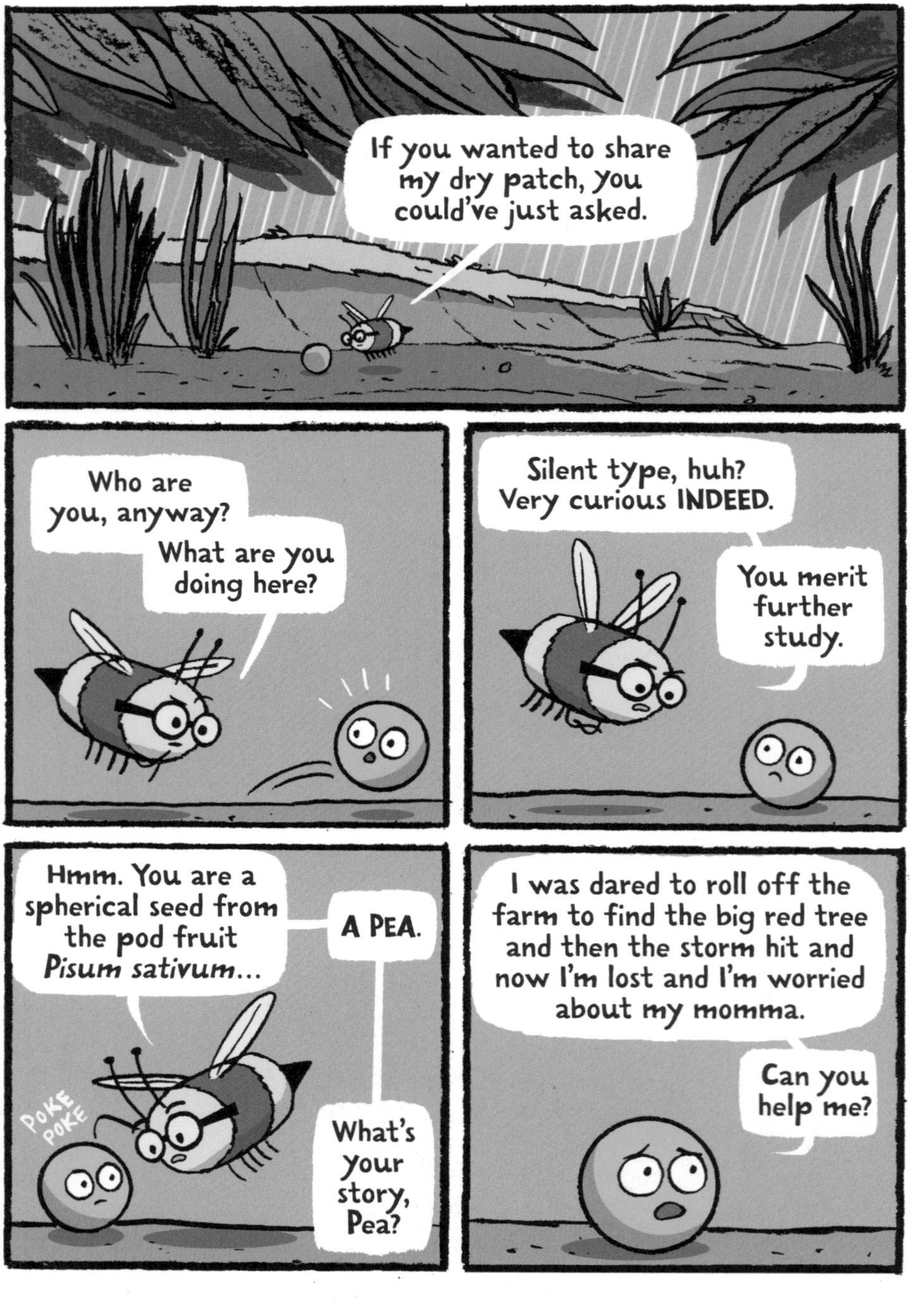
If you wanted to share my dry patch, you could've just asked.
Who are you, anyway?
What are you doing here?
Silent type, huh? Very curious INDEED.
You merit further study.
Hmm. You are a spherical seed from the pod fruit *Pisum sativum*...
A PEA.
What's your story, Pea?
POKE POKE
I was dared to roll off the farm to find the big red tree and then the storm hit and now I'm lost and I'm worried about my momma.
Can you help me?

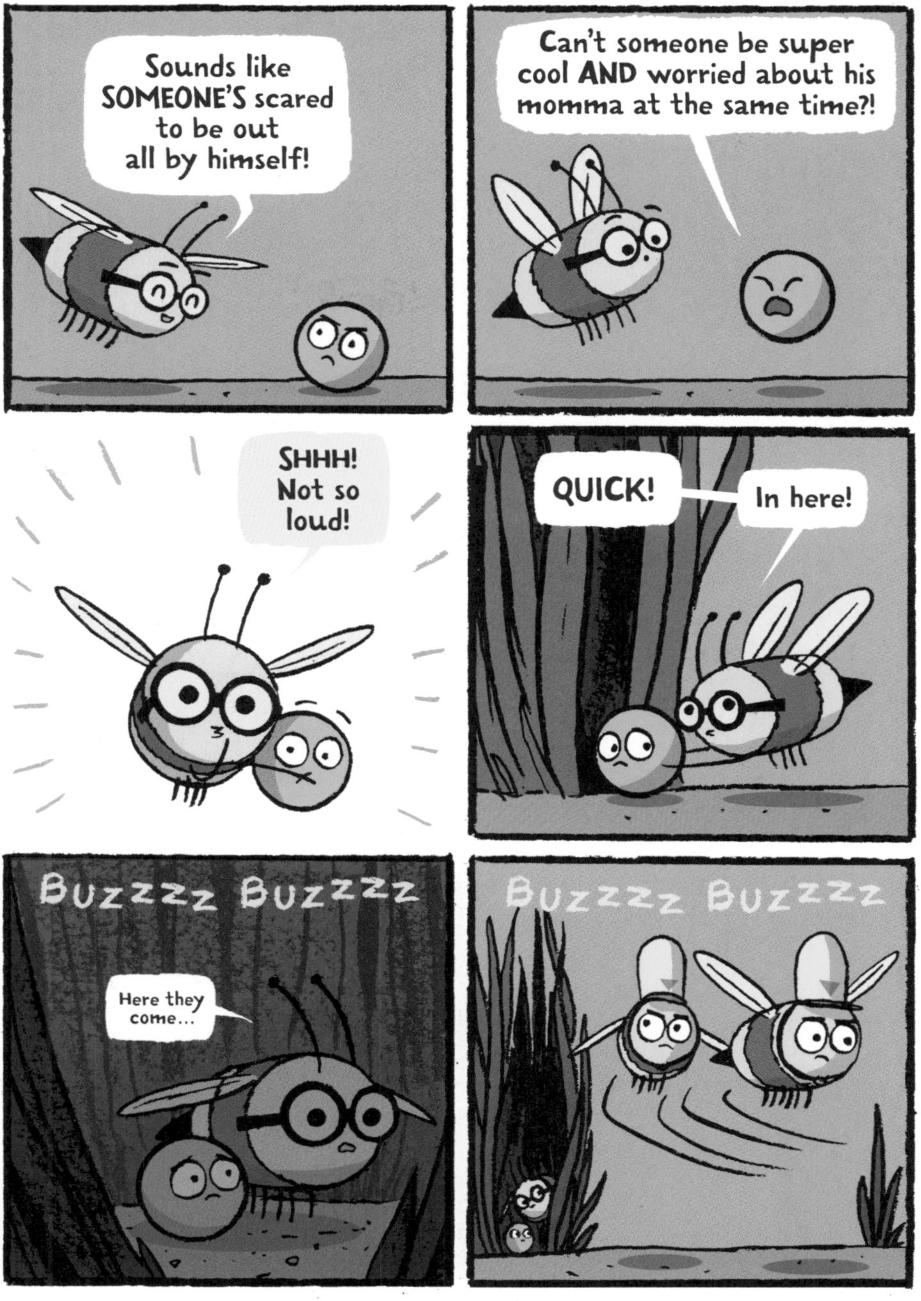
Sounds like SOMEONE'S scared to be out all by himself!
Can't someone be super cool AND worried about his momma at the same time?!
SHHH! Not so loud!
QUICK!
In here!
BUZZZZ BUZZZZ
Here they come...
BUZZZZ BUZZZZ

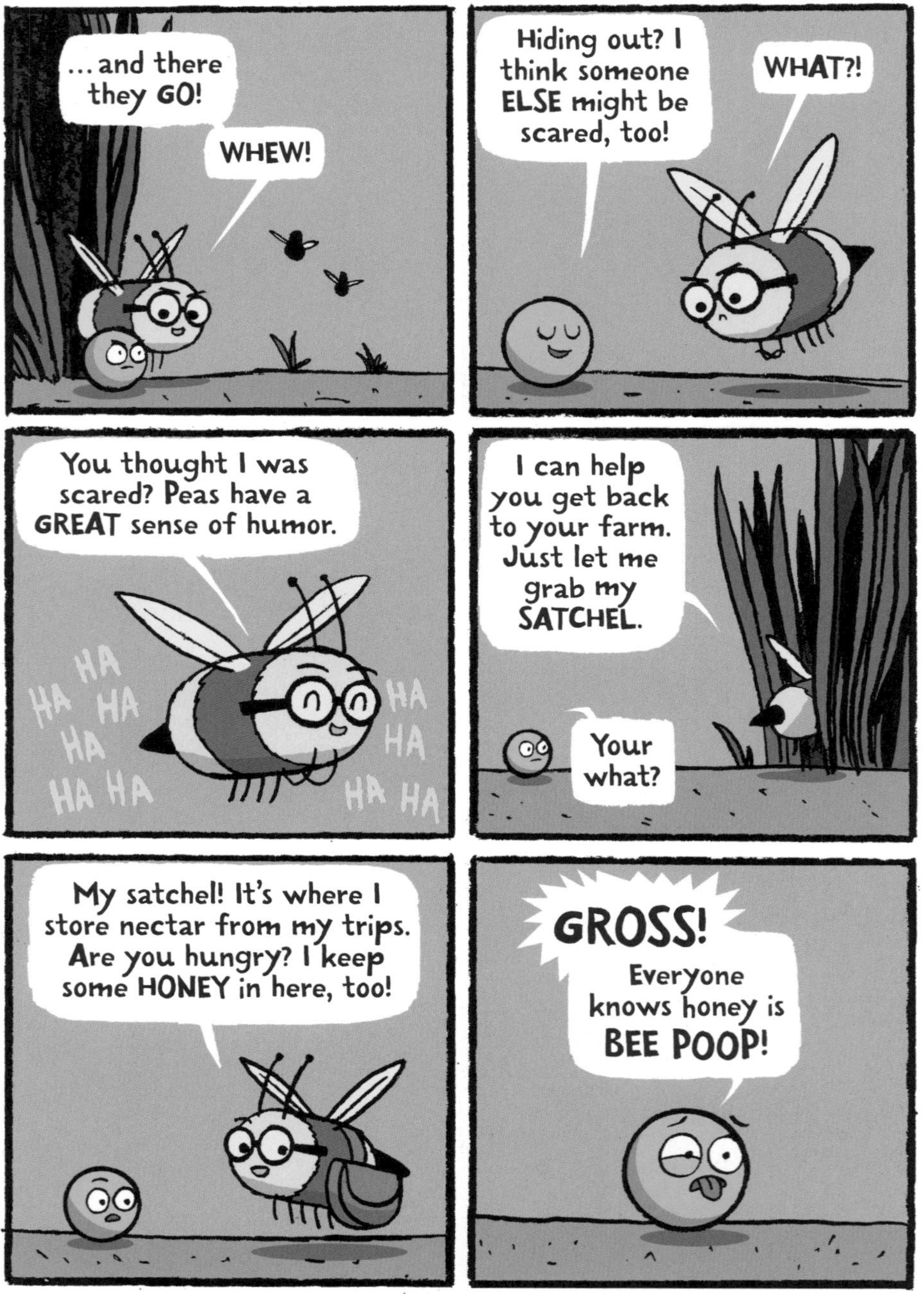
...and there they GO!
WHEW!
Hiding out? I think someone ELSE might be scared, too!
WHAT?!
You thought I was scared? Peas have a GREAT sense of humor.
HA HA HA HA HA HA HA HA HA HA HA HA
I can help you get back to your farm. Just let me grab my SATCHEL.
Your what?
My satchel! It's where I store nectar from my trips. Are you hungry? I keep some HONEY in here, too!
GROSS!
Everyone knows honey is BEE POOP!

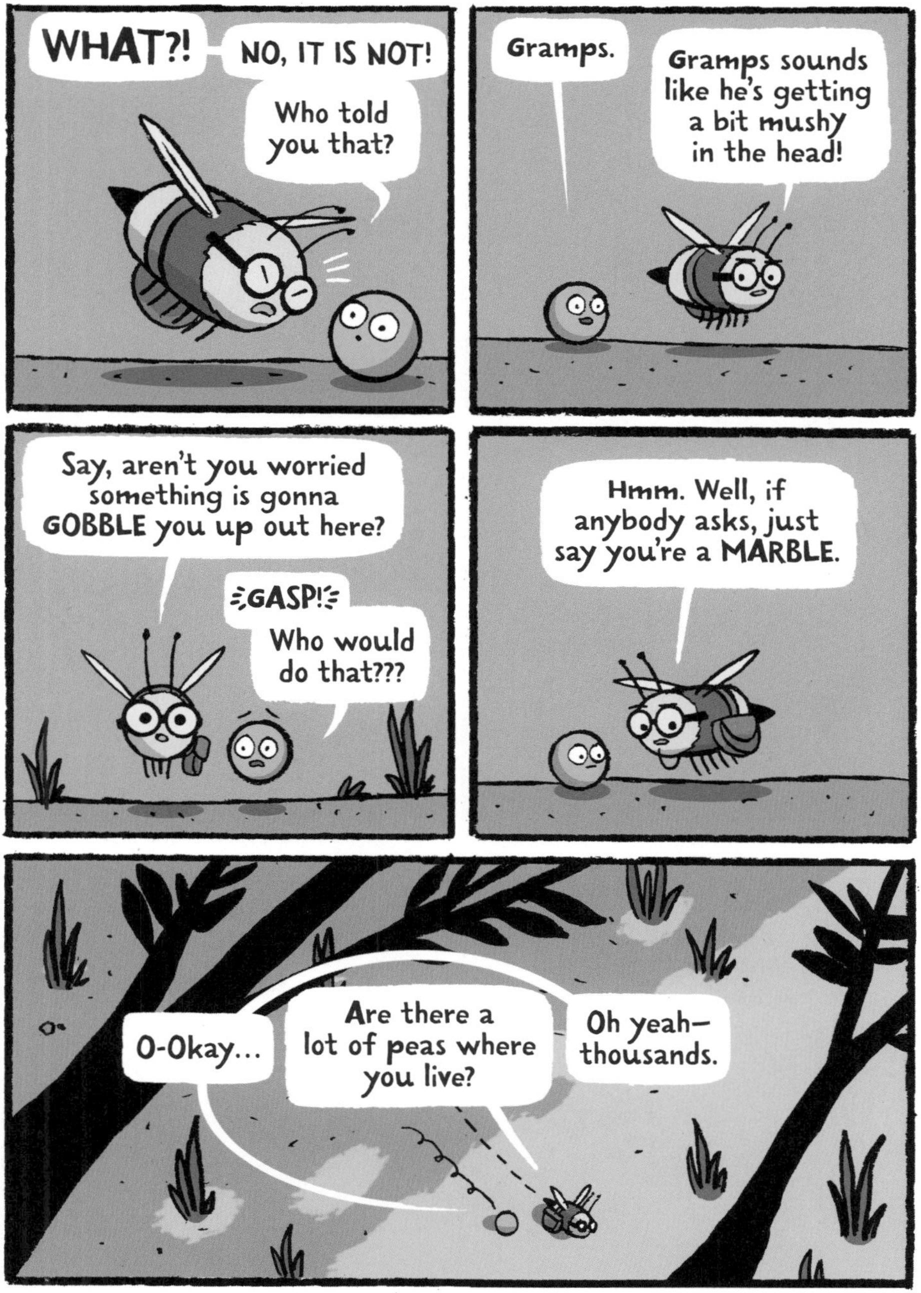
WHAT?!
NO, IT IS NOT!
Who told you that?
Gramps.
Gramps sounds like he's getting a bit mushy in the head!
Say, aren't you worried something is gonna GOBBLE you up out here?
GASP!
Who would do that???
Hmm. Well, if anybody asks, just say you're a MARBLE.
O-Okay...
Are there a lot of peas where you live?
Oh yeah— thousands.

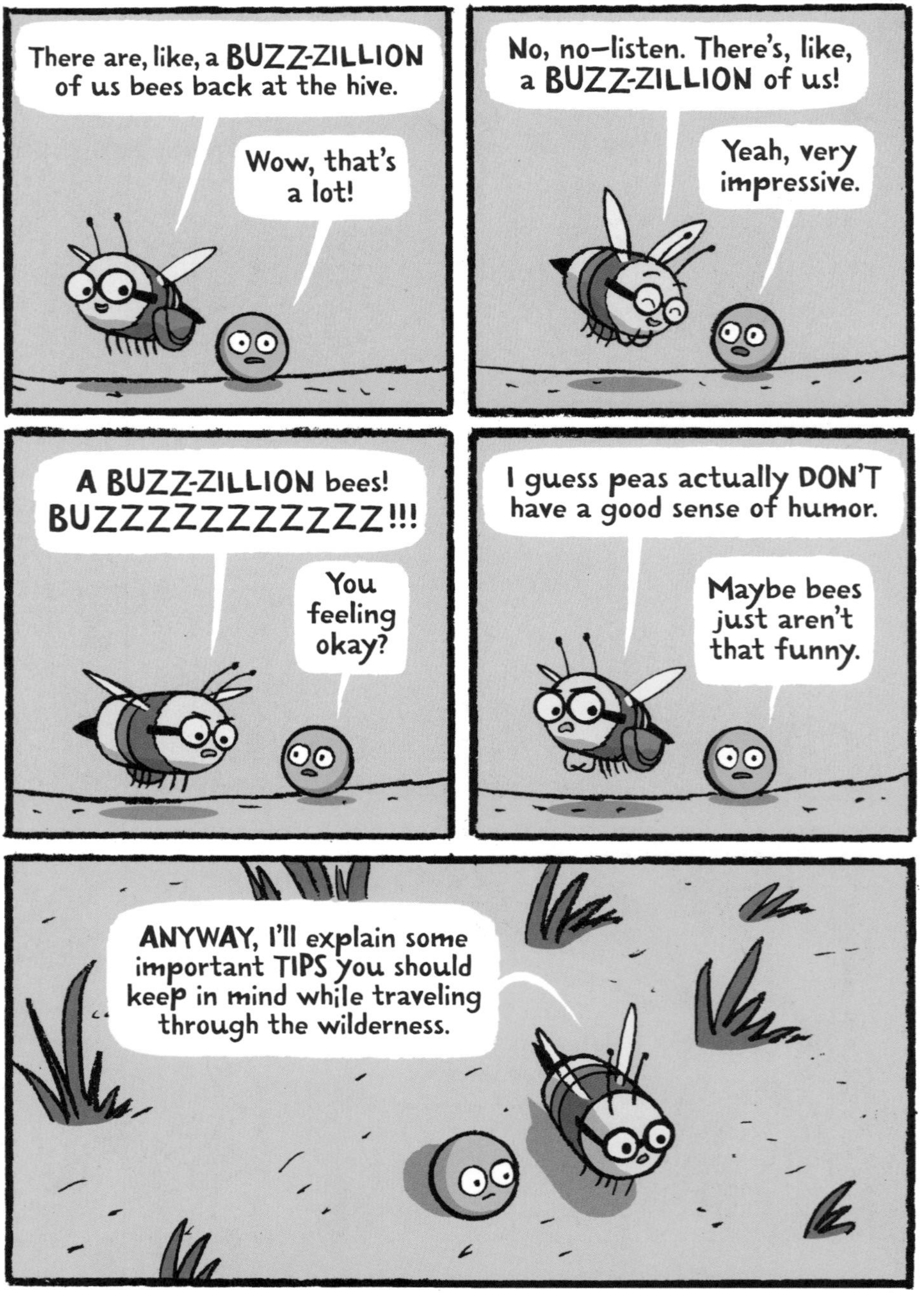
There are, like, a BUZZ-ZILLION of us bees back at the hive.
Wow, that's a lot!
No, no—listen. There's, like, a BUZZ-ZILLION of us!
Yeah, very impressive.
A BUZZ-ZILLION bees! BUZZZZZZZZZZZZ!!!
You feeling okay?
I guess peas actually DON'T have a good sense of humor.
Maybe bees just aren't that funny.
ANYWAY, I'll explain some important TIPS you should keep in mind while traveling through the wilderness.

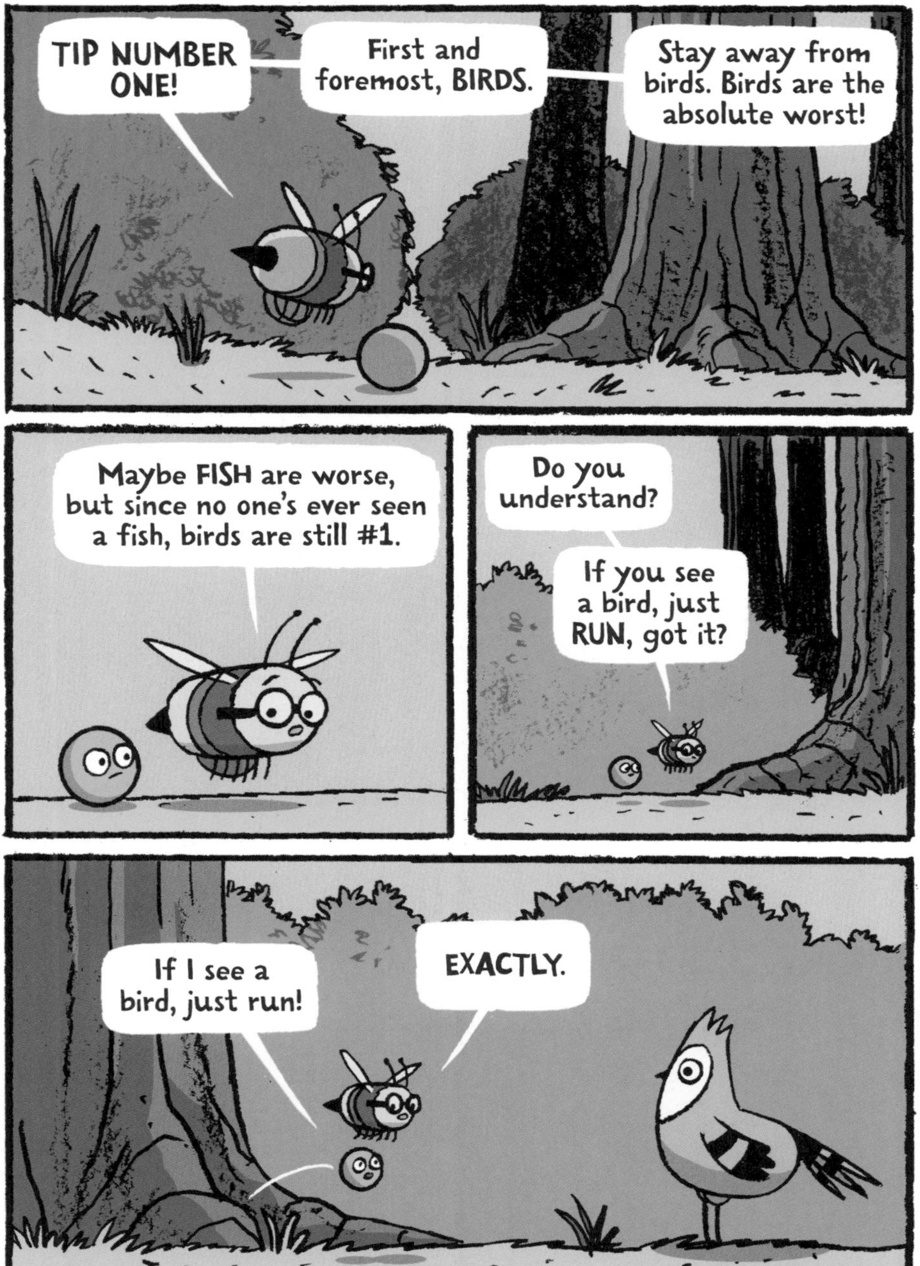
TIP NUMBER ONE!
First and foremost, BIRDS.
Stay away from birds. Birds are the absolute worst!
Maybe FISH are worse, but since no one's ever seen a fish, birds are still #1.
Do you understand?
If you see a bird, just RUN, got it?
If I see a bird, just run!
EXACTLY.

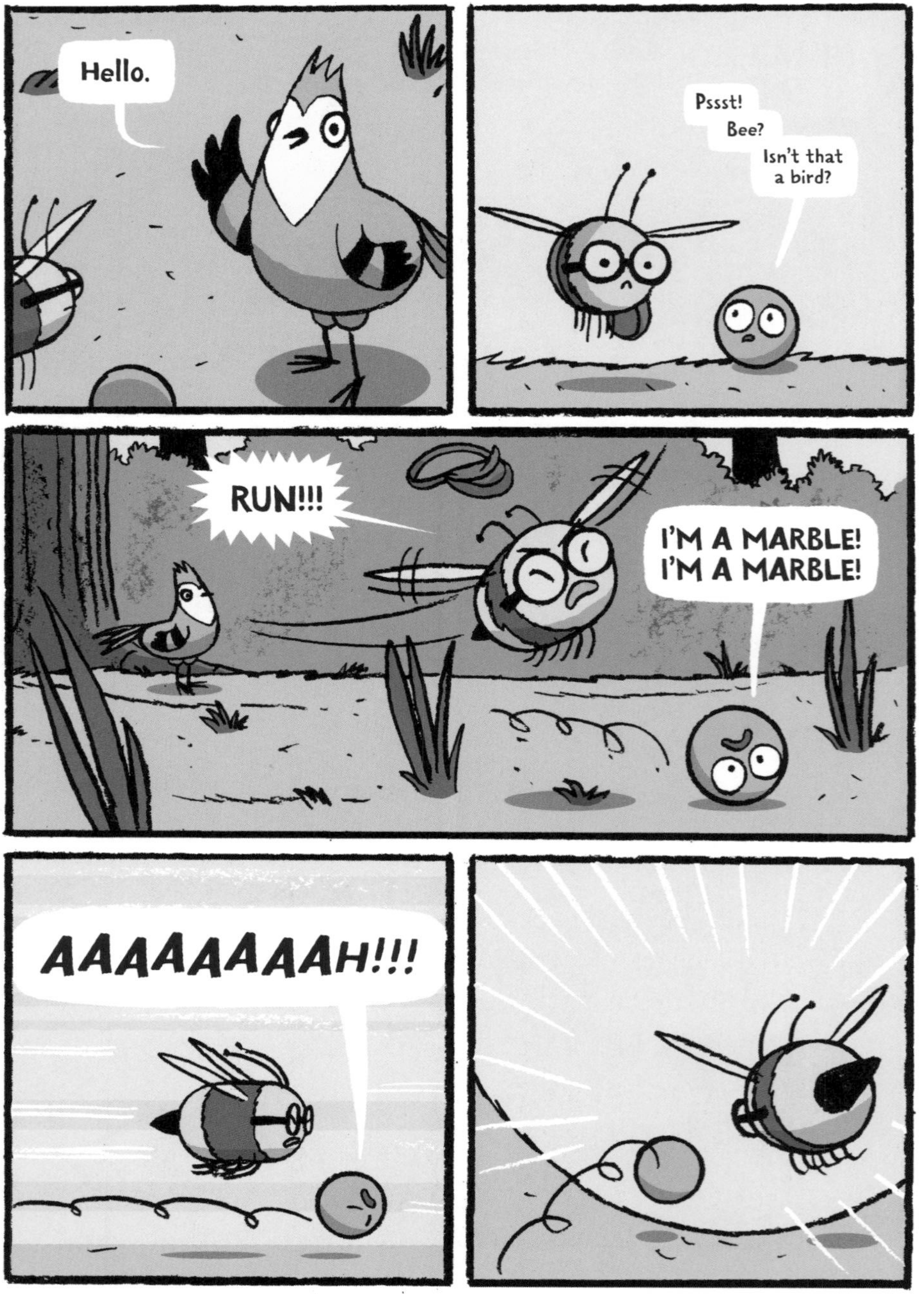
Hello.
Pssst!
Bee?
Isn't that a bird?
RUN!!!
I'M A MARBLE! I'M A MARBLE!
AAAAAAAAH!!!

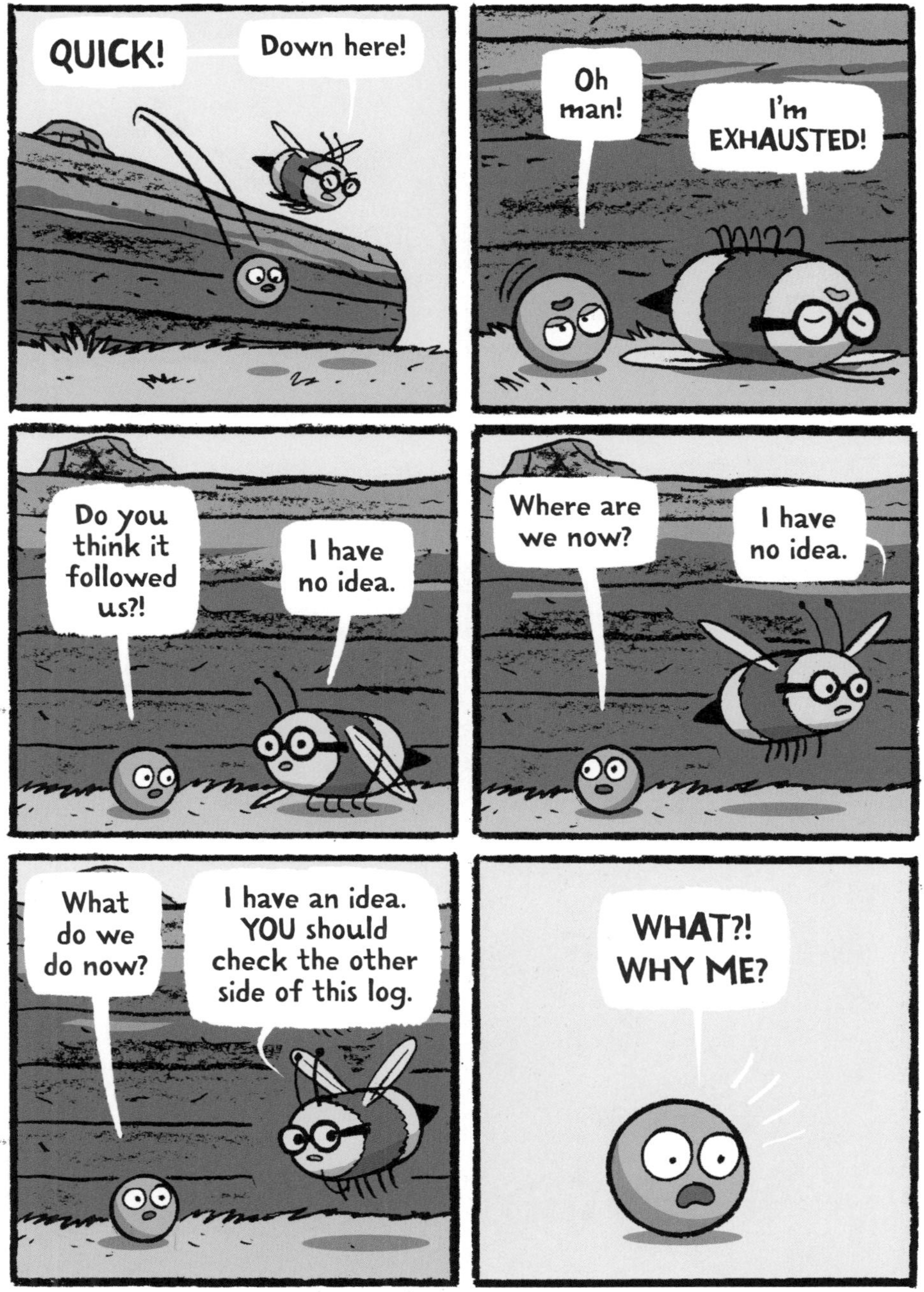
QUICK!
Down here!
Oh man!
I'm EXHAUSTED!
Do you think it followed us?!
I have no idea.
Where are we now?
I have no idea.
What do we do now?
I have an idea. YOU should check the other side of this log.
WHAT?! WHY ME?

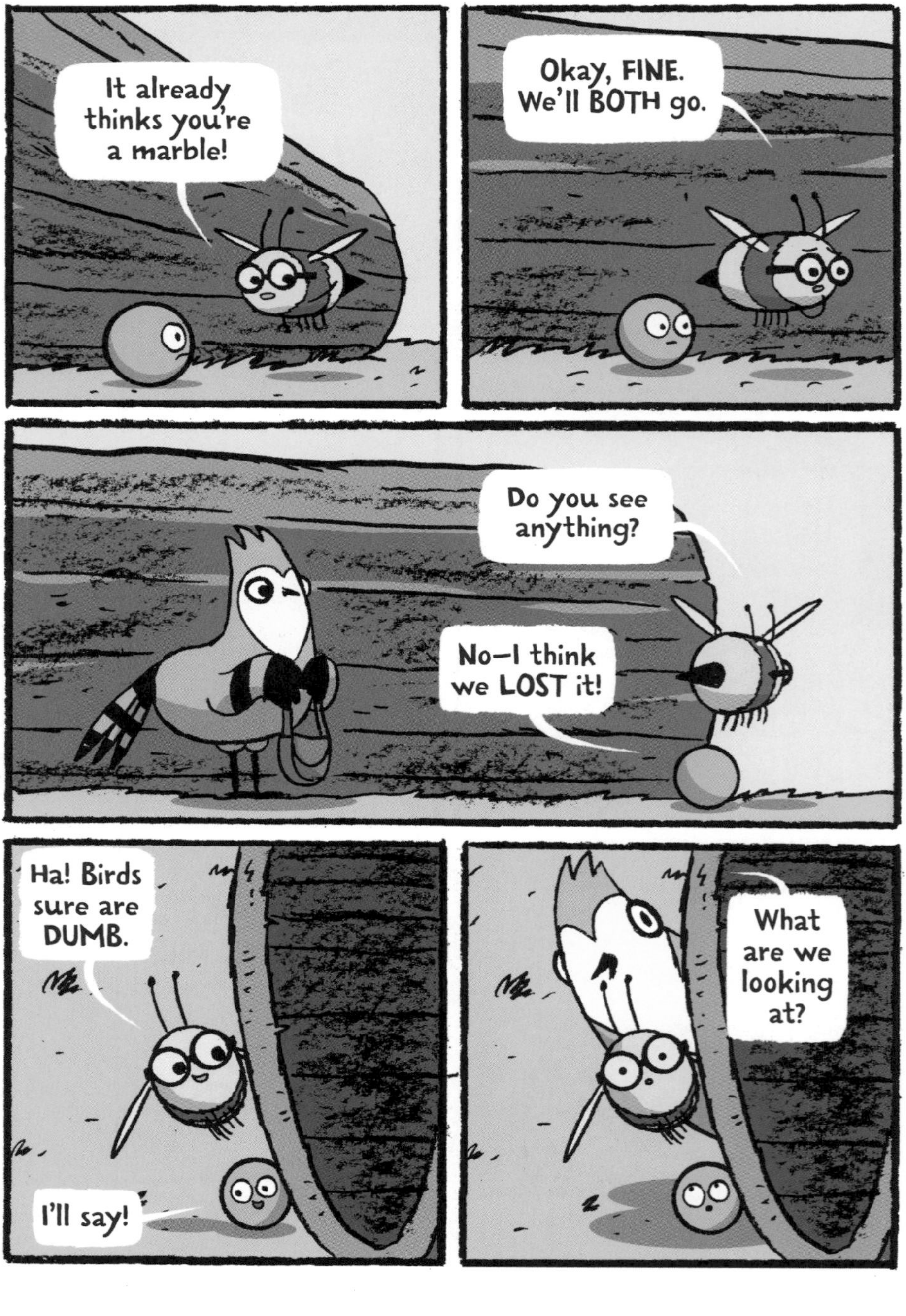
It already thinks you're a marble!
Okay, FINE. We'll BOTH go.
Do you see anything?
No—I think we LOST it!
Ha! Birds sure are DUMB.
I'll say!
What are we looking at?

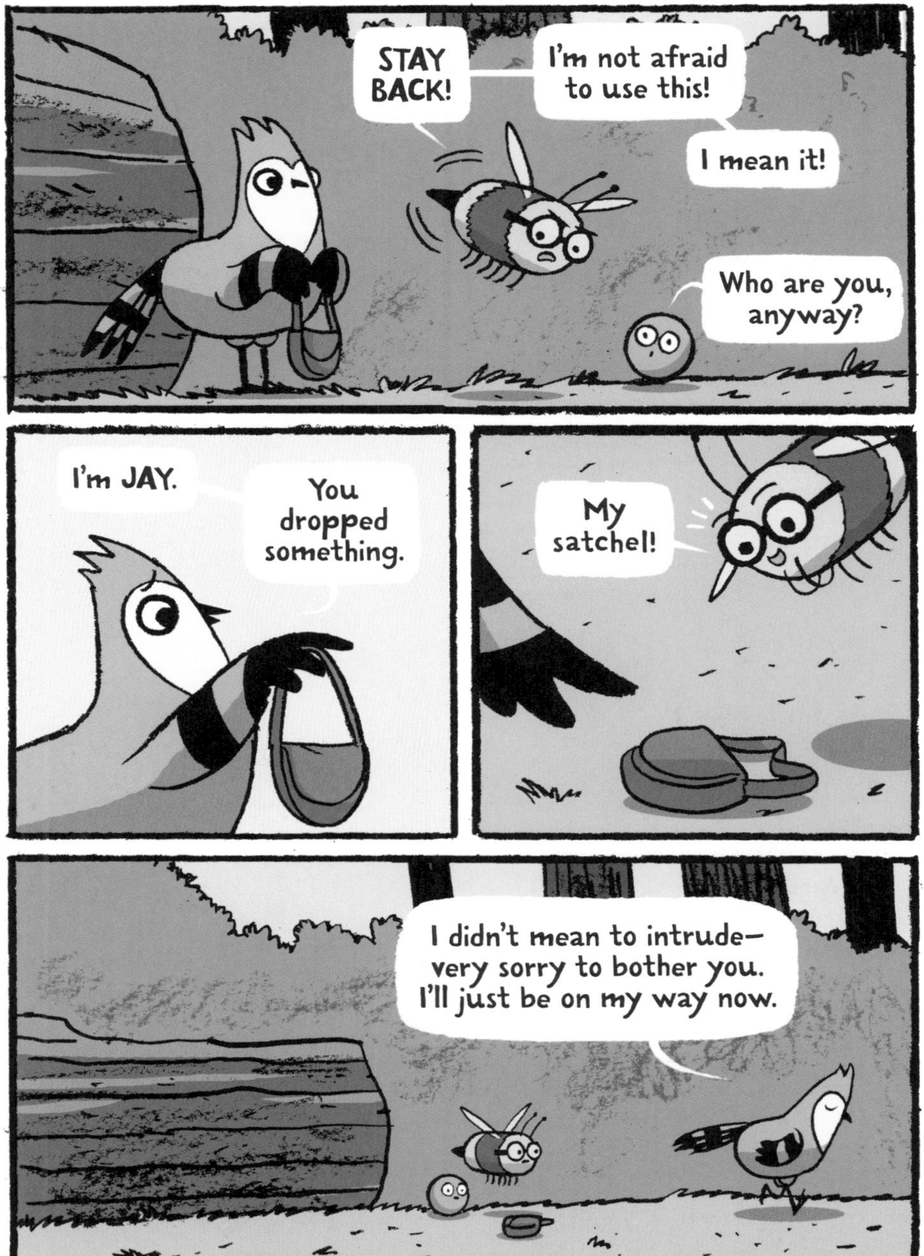
STAY BACK!
I'm not afraid to use this!
I mean it!
Who are you, anyway?
I'm JAY.
You dropped something.
My satchel!
I didn't mean to intrude—very sorry to bother you. I'll just be on my way now.

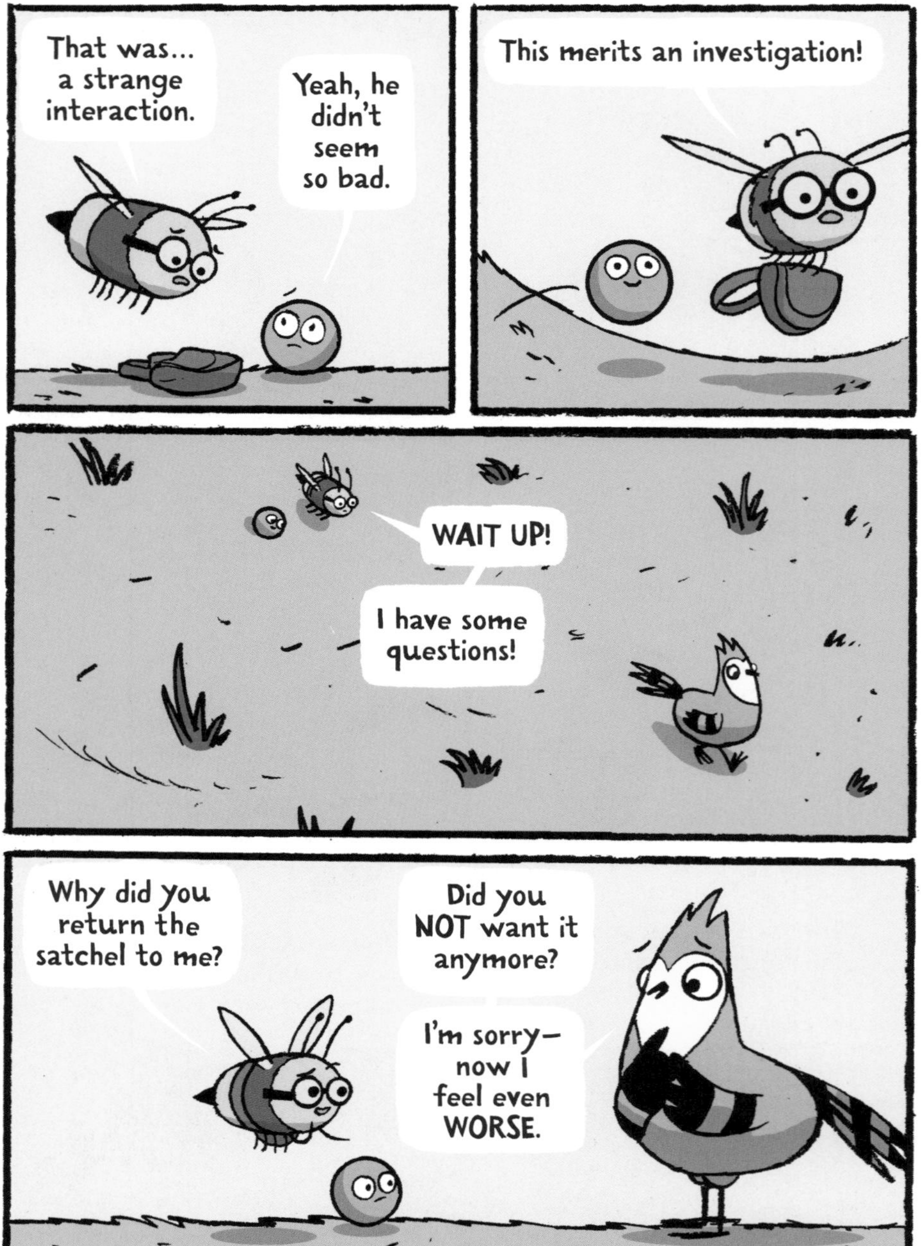

That was... a strange interaction.
Yeah, he didn't seem so bad.
This merits an investigation!
WAIT UP!
I have some questions!
Why did you return the satchel to me?
Did you NOT want it anymore?
I'm sorry—now I feel even WORSE.

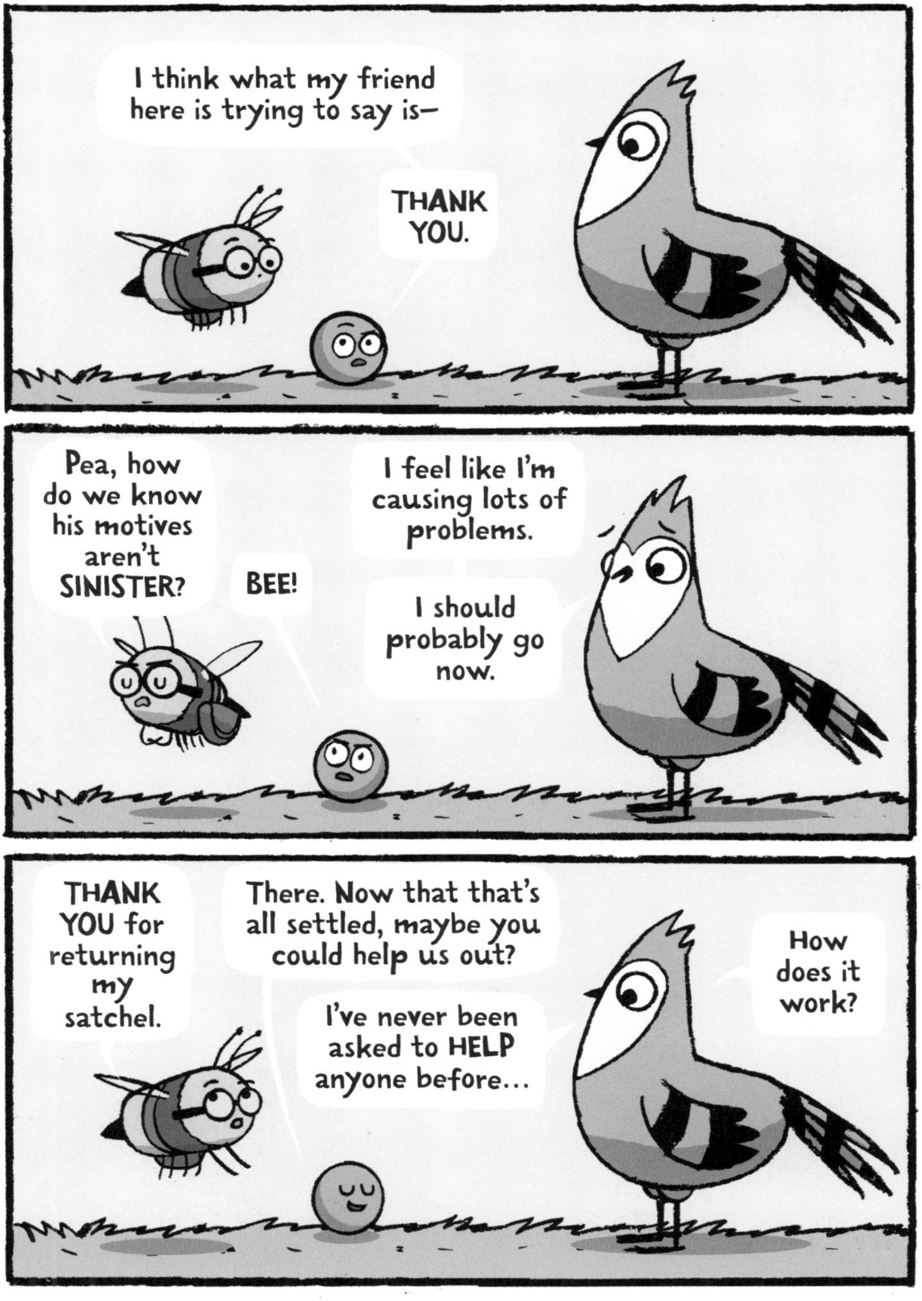
I think what my friend here is trying to say is—
THANK YOU.
Pea, how do we know his motives aren't SINISTER?
BEE!
I feel like I'm causing lots of problems.
I should probably go now.
THANK YOU for returning my satchel.
There. Now that that's all settled, maybe you could help us out?
I've never been asked to HELP anyone before...
How does it work?

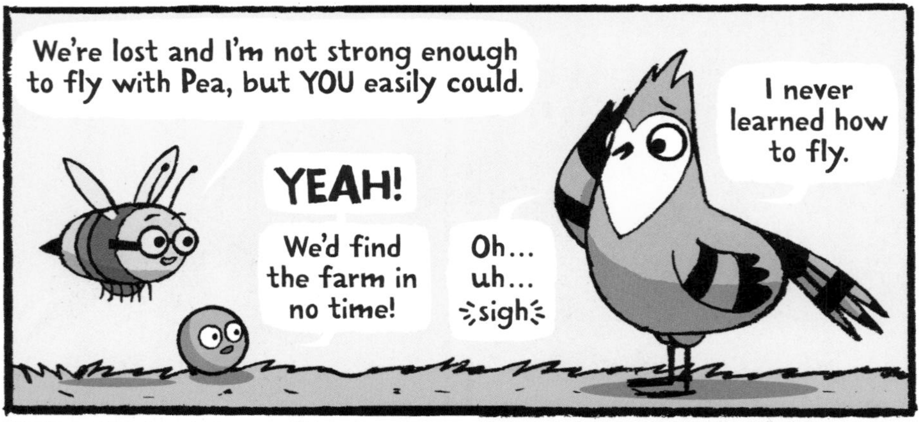
We're lost and I'm not strong enough to fly with Pea, but YOU easily could.
YEAH!
We'd find the farm in no time!
Oh... uh... sigh
I never learned how to fly.

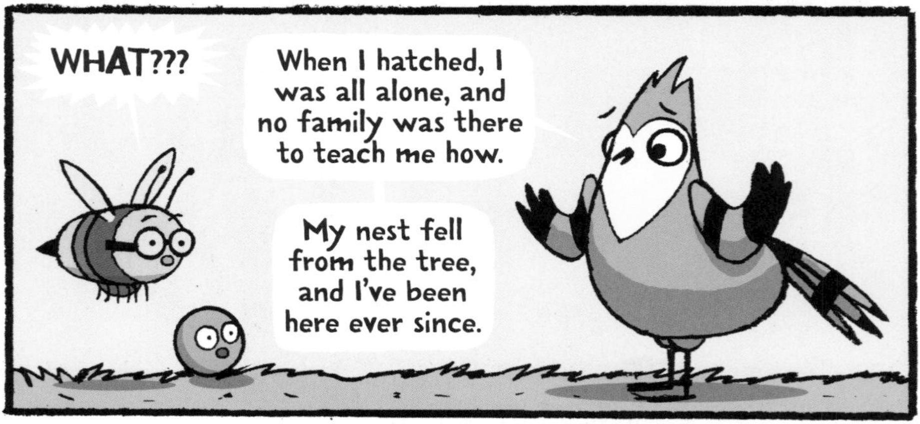
WHAT???
When I hatched, I was all alone, and no family was there to teach me how.
My nest fell from the tree, and I've been here ever since.

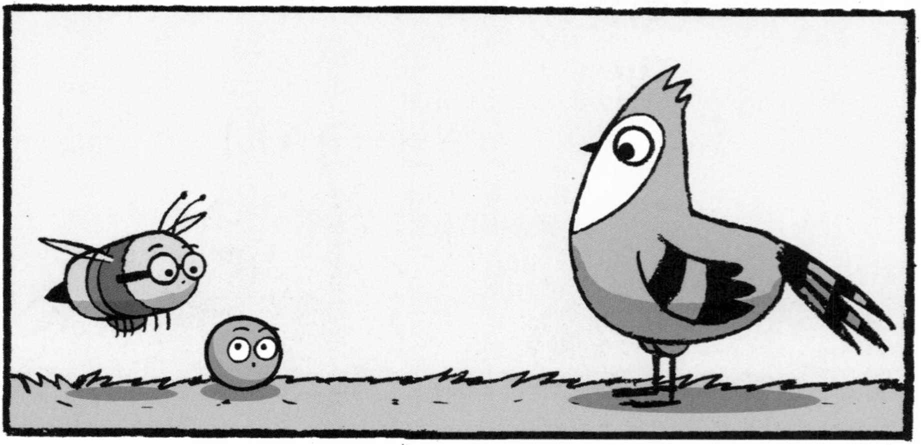

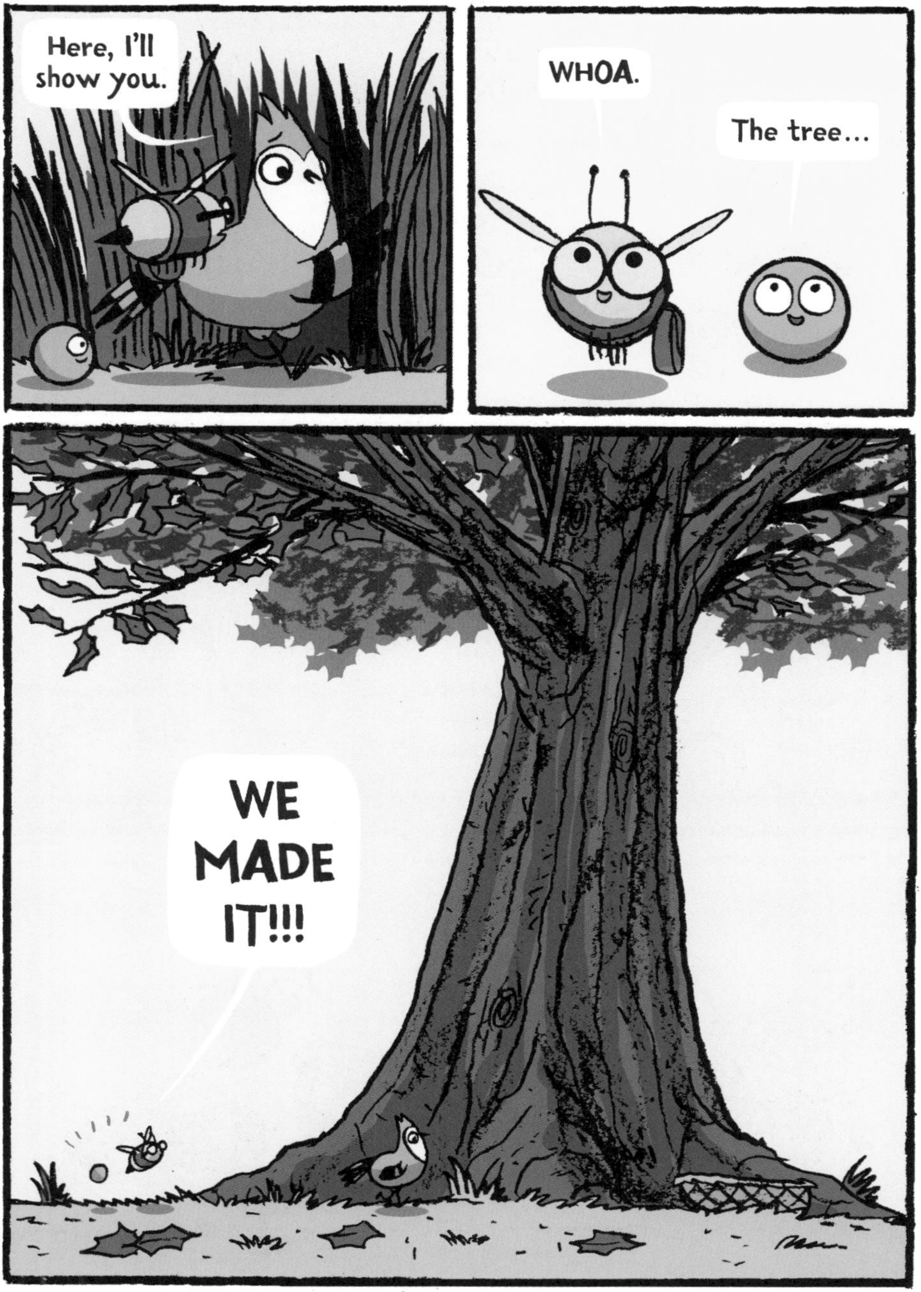
Here, I'll show you.
WHOA.
The tree...
WE MADE IT!!!

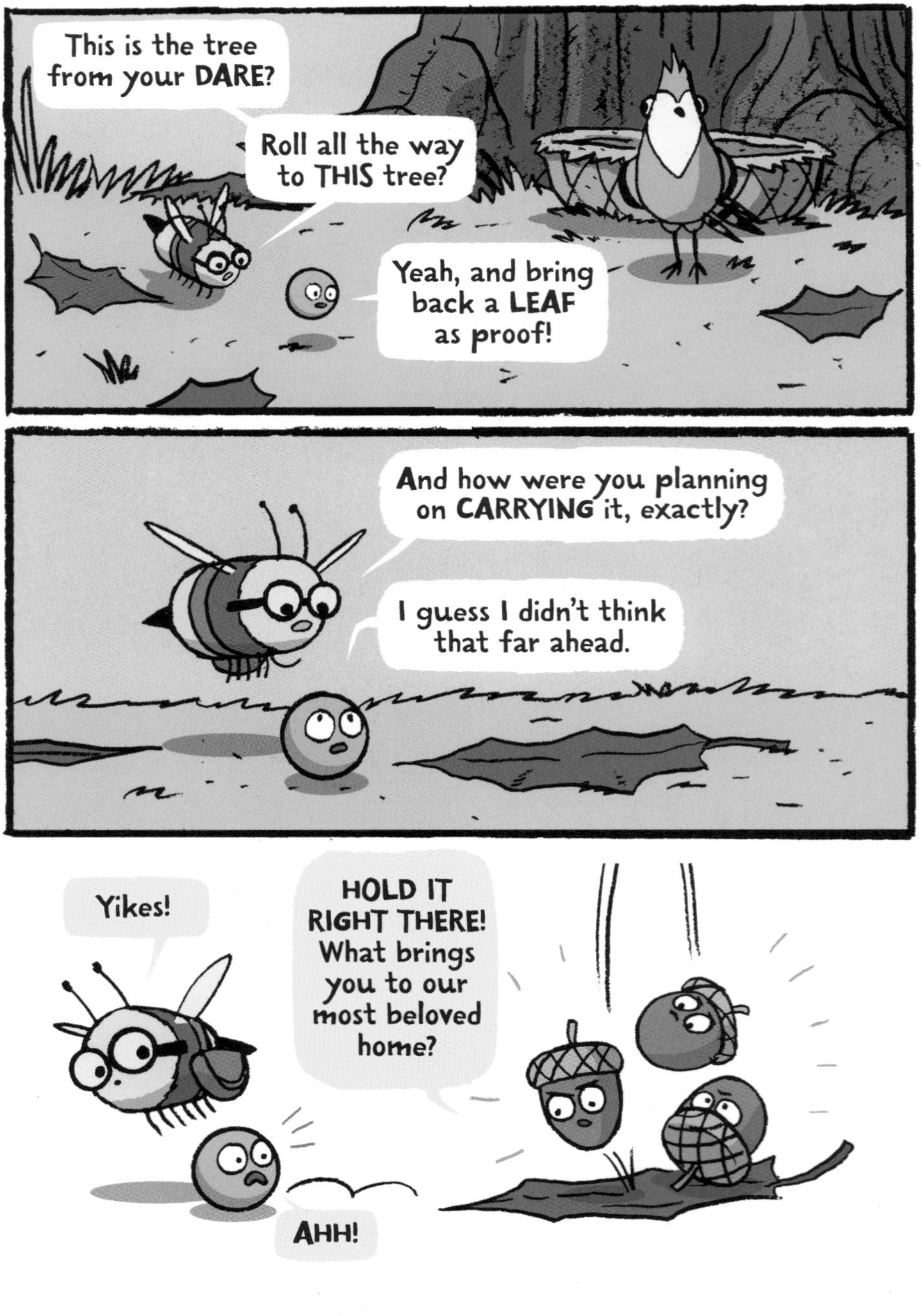
This is the tree from your DARE?
Roll all the way to THIS tree?
Yeah, and bring back a LEAF as proof!
And how were you planning on CARRYING it, exactly?
I guess I didn't think that far ahead.
Yikes!
HOLD IT RIGHT THERE! What brings you to our most beloved home?
AHH!

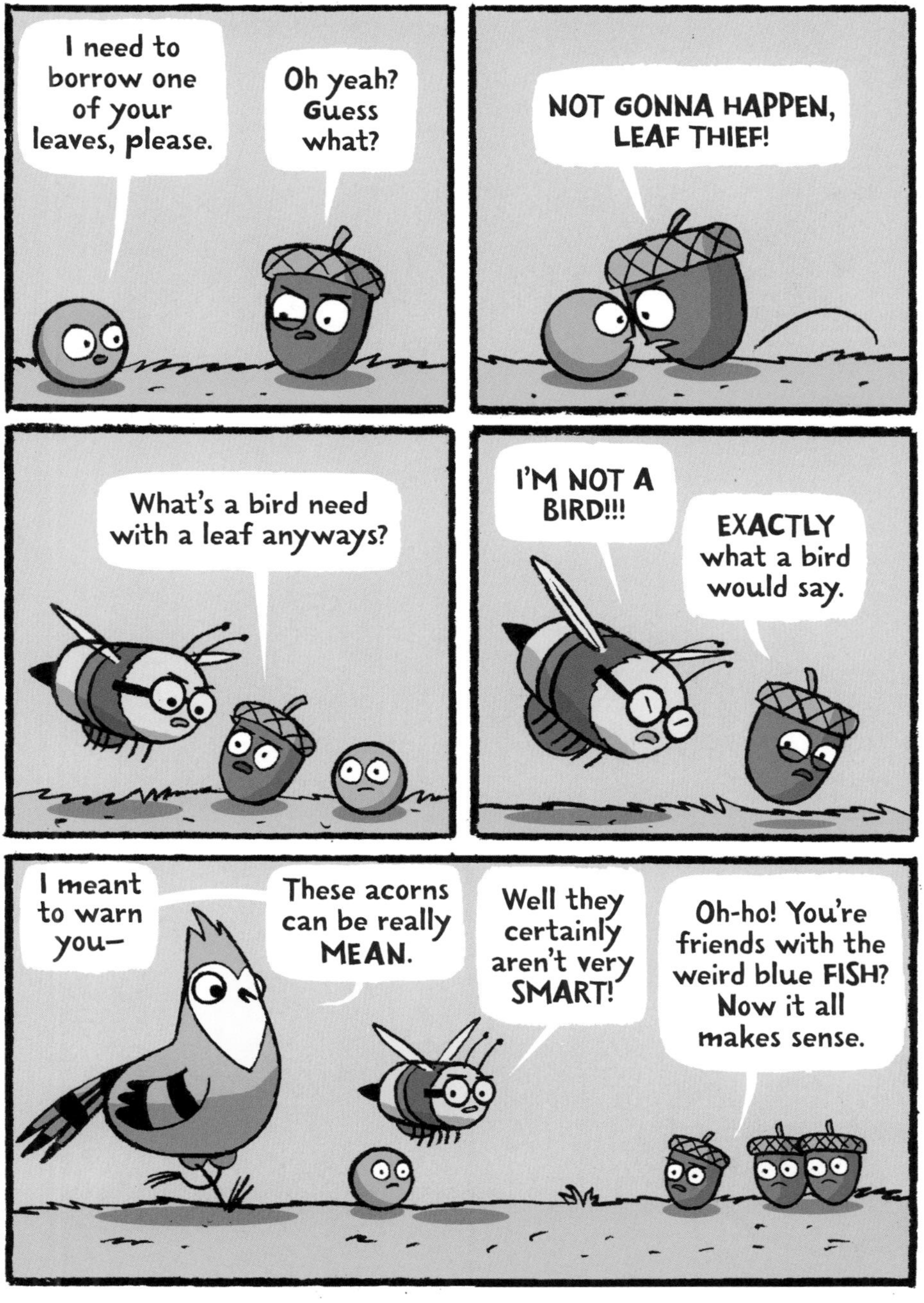
I need to borrow one of your leaves, please.
Oh yeah? Guess what?
NOT GONNA HAPPEN, LEAF THIEF!
What's a bird need with a leaf anyways?
I'M NOT A BIRD!!!
EXACTLY what a bird would say.
I meant to warn you—
These acorns can be really MEAN.
Well they certainly aren't very SMART!
Oh-ho! You're friends with the weird blue FISH? Now it all makes sense.

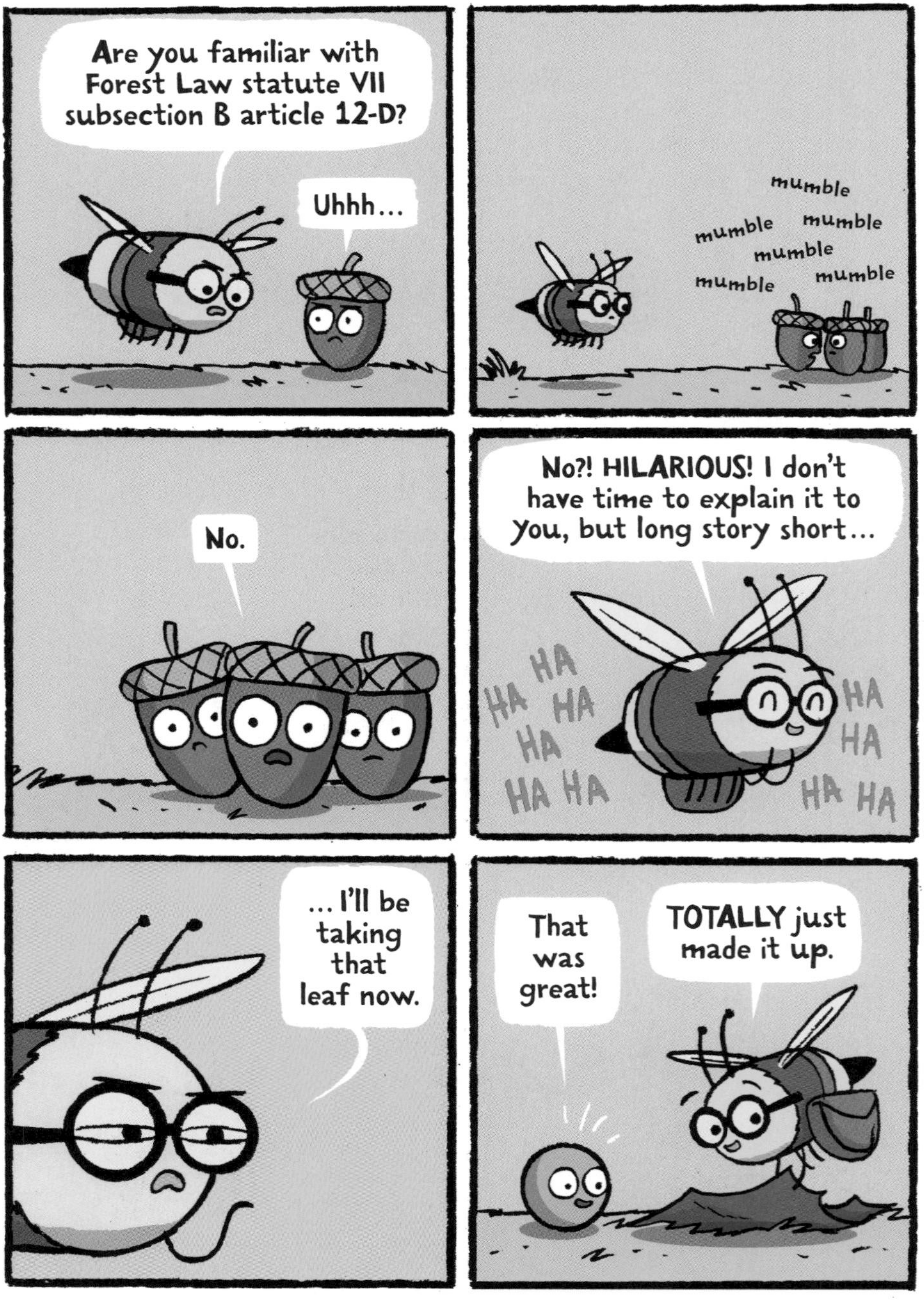
Are you familiar with Forest Law statute VII subsection B article 12-D?
Uhhh...
mumble
mumble mumble
mumble
mumble mumble
No.
No?! HILARIOUS! I don't have time to explain it to you, but long story short...
HA HA HA HA HA HA HA
HA HA HA HA
...I'll be taking that leaf now.
That was great!
TOTALLY just made it up.

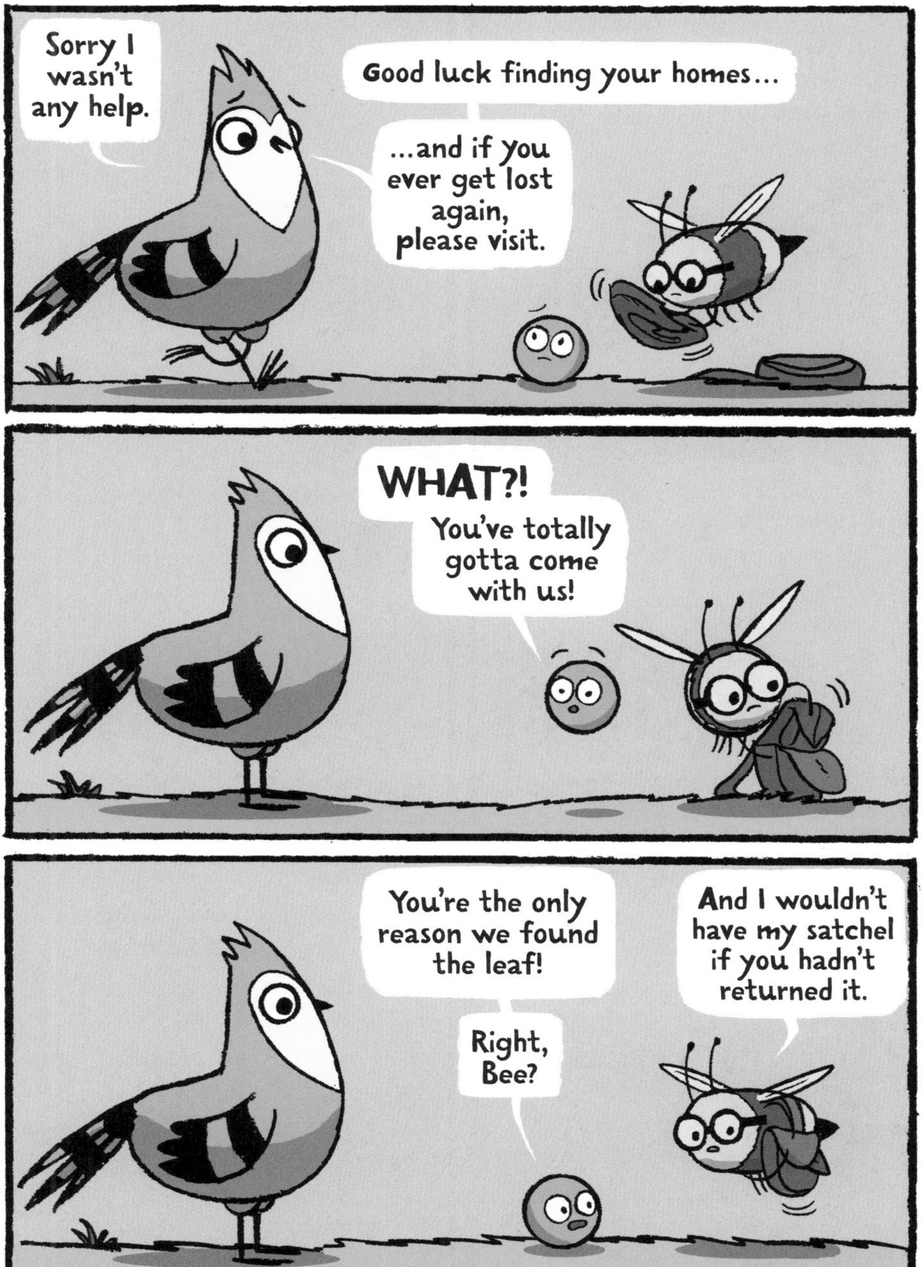
Sorry I wasn't any help.
Good luck finding your homes...
...and if you ever get lost again, please visit.
WHAT?!
You've totally gotta come with us!
You're the only reason we found the leaf!
Right, Bee?
And I wouldn't have my satchel if you hadn't returned it.

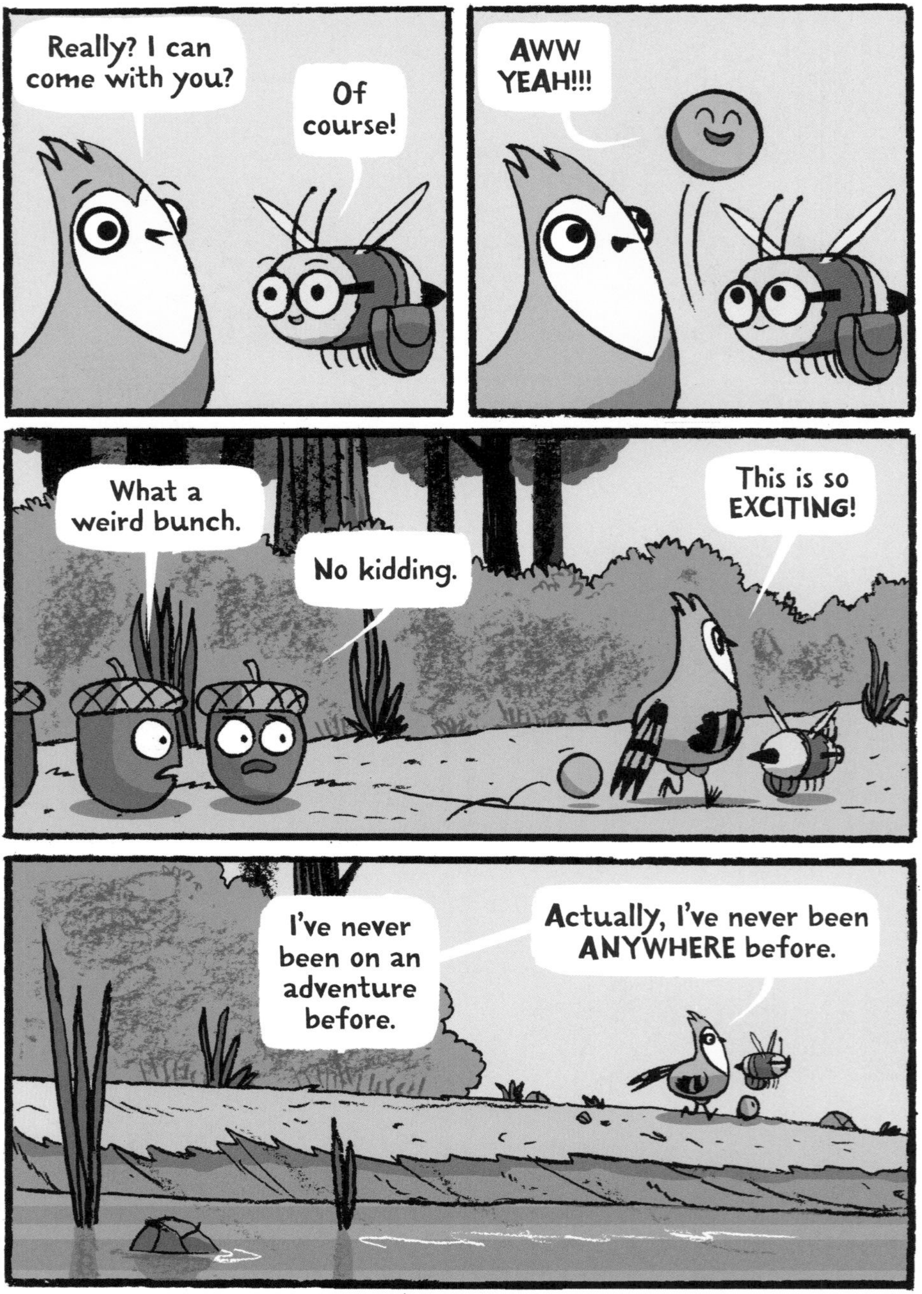

Really? I can come with you?
Of course!
AWW YEAH!!!
What a weird bunch.
No kidding.
This is so EXCITING!
I've never been on an adventure before.
Actually, I've never been ANYWHERE before.

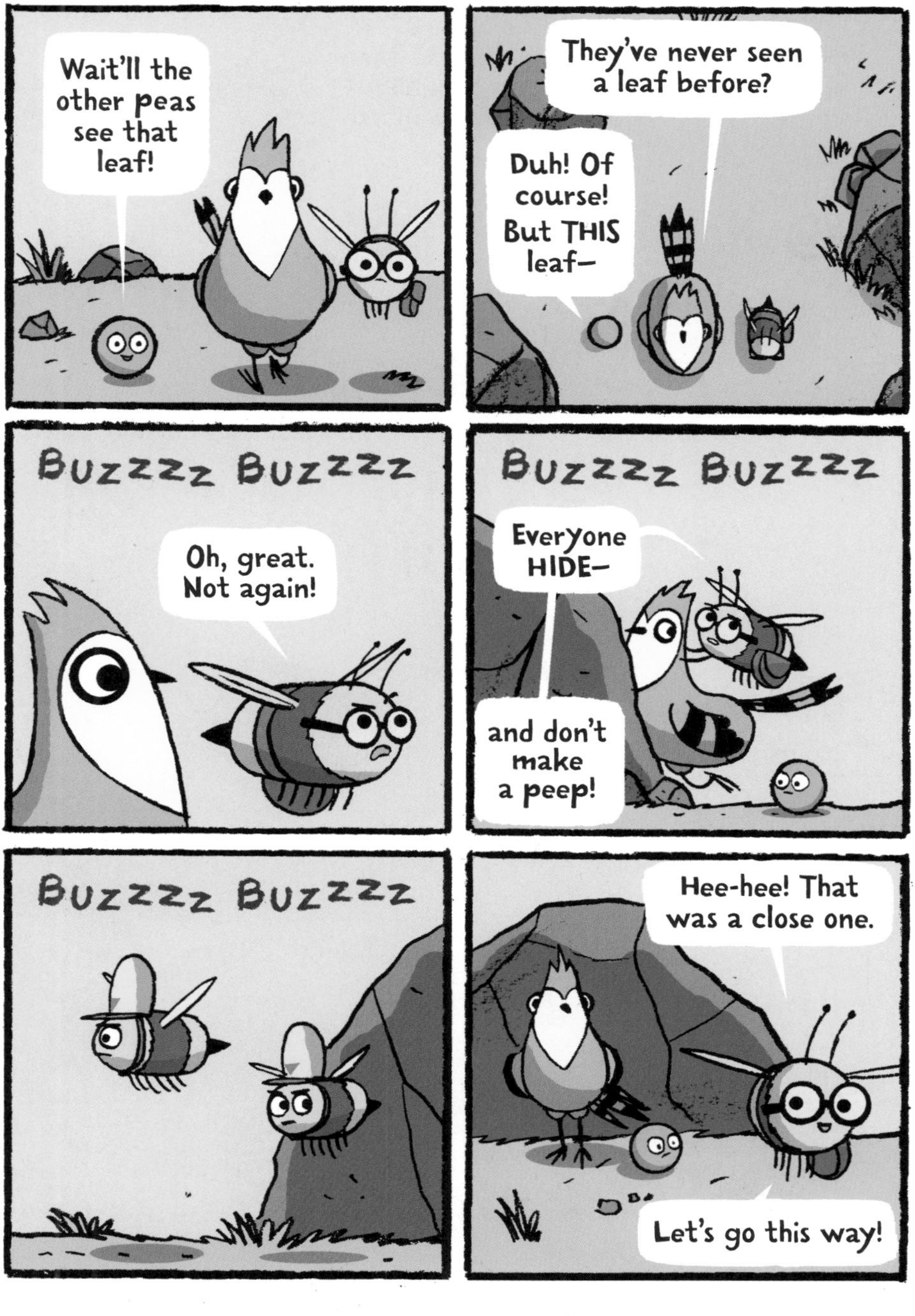
Wait'll the other peas see that leaf!
They've never seen a leaf before?
Duh! Of course! But THIS leaf—
BUZZZZ BUZZZZ
Oh, great. Not again!
BUZZZZ BUZZZZ
Everyone HIDE—
and don't make a peep!
BUZZZZ BUZZZZ
Hee-hee! That was a close one.
Let's go this way!

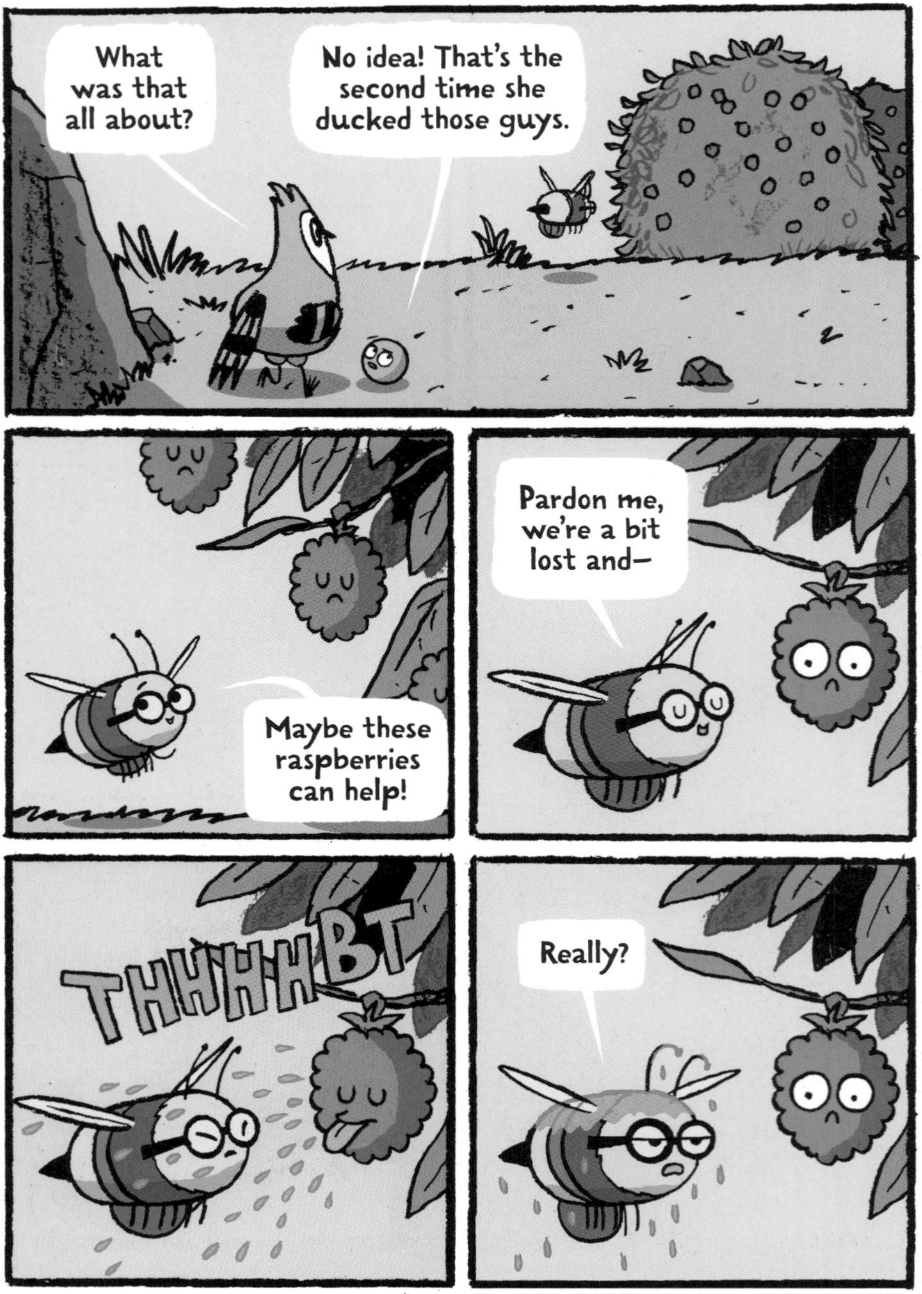
What was that all about?
No idea! That's the second time she ducked those guys.
Maybe these raspberries can help!
Pardon me, we're a bit lost and—
THHHHBT
Really?

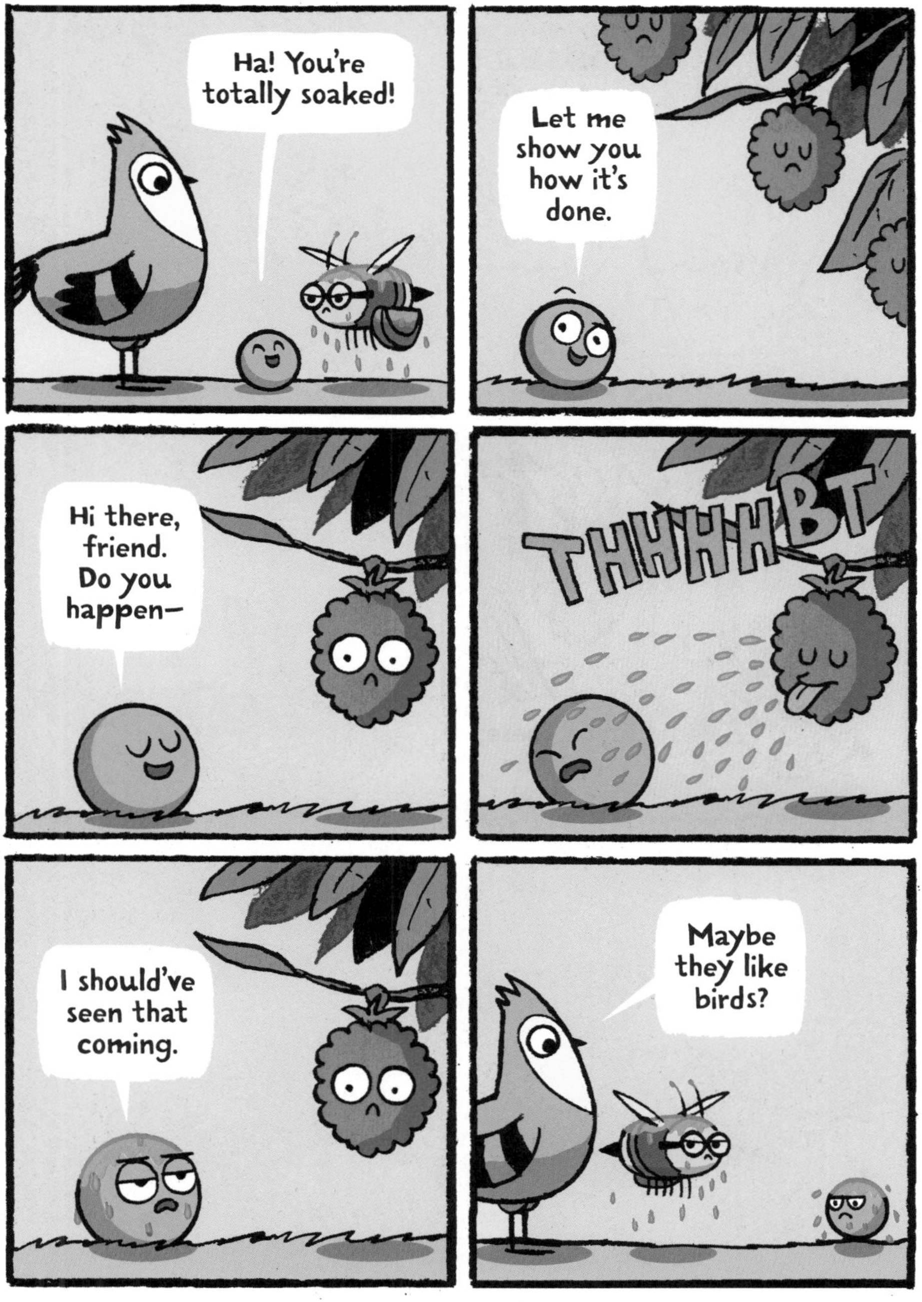
Ha! You're totally soaked!
Let me show you how it's done.
Hi there, friend. Do you happen—
THHHHBT
I should've seen that coming.
Maybe they like birds?

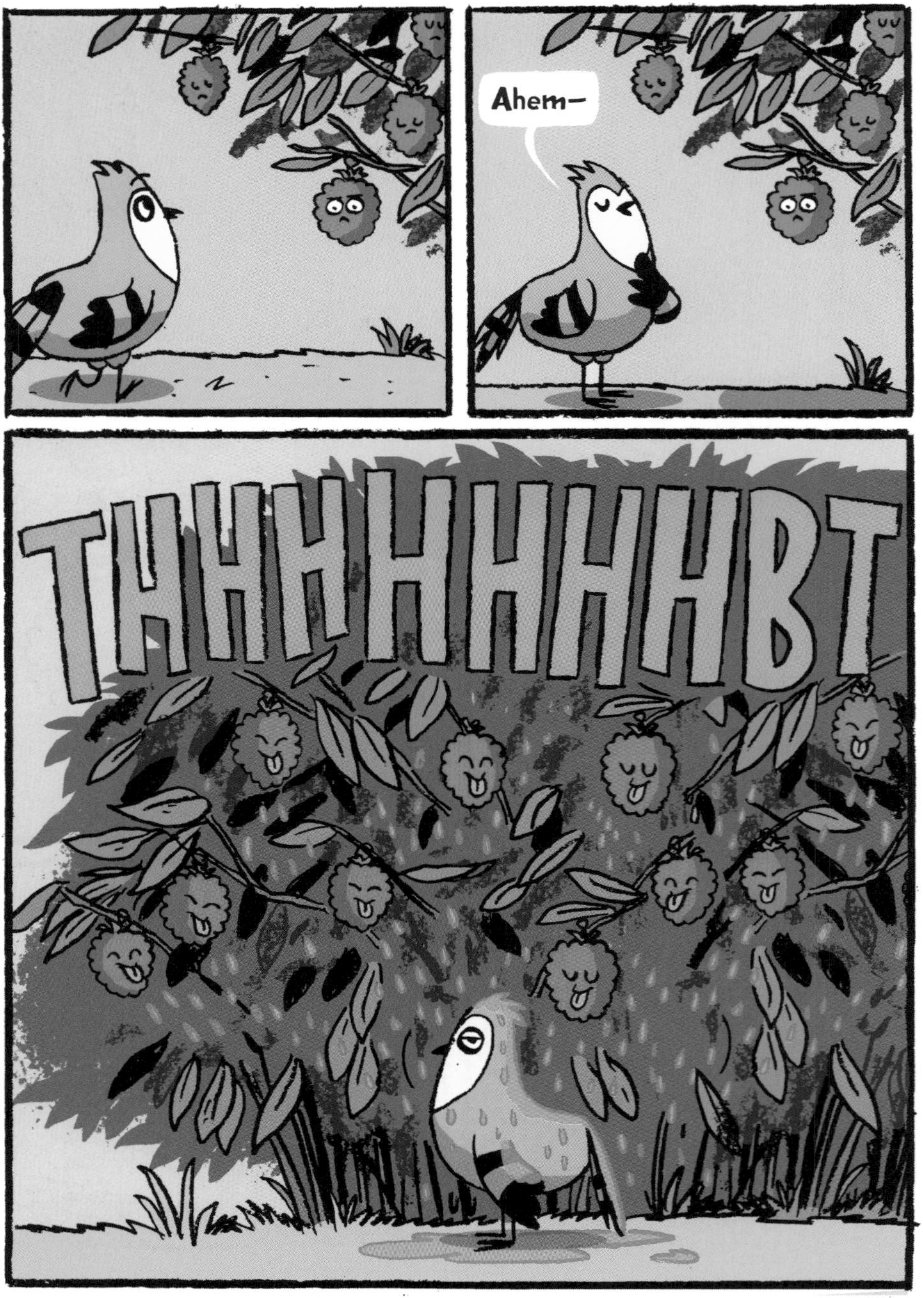
Ahem–
THHHHHHBT

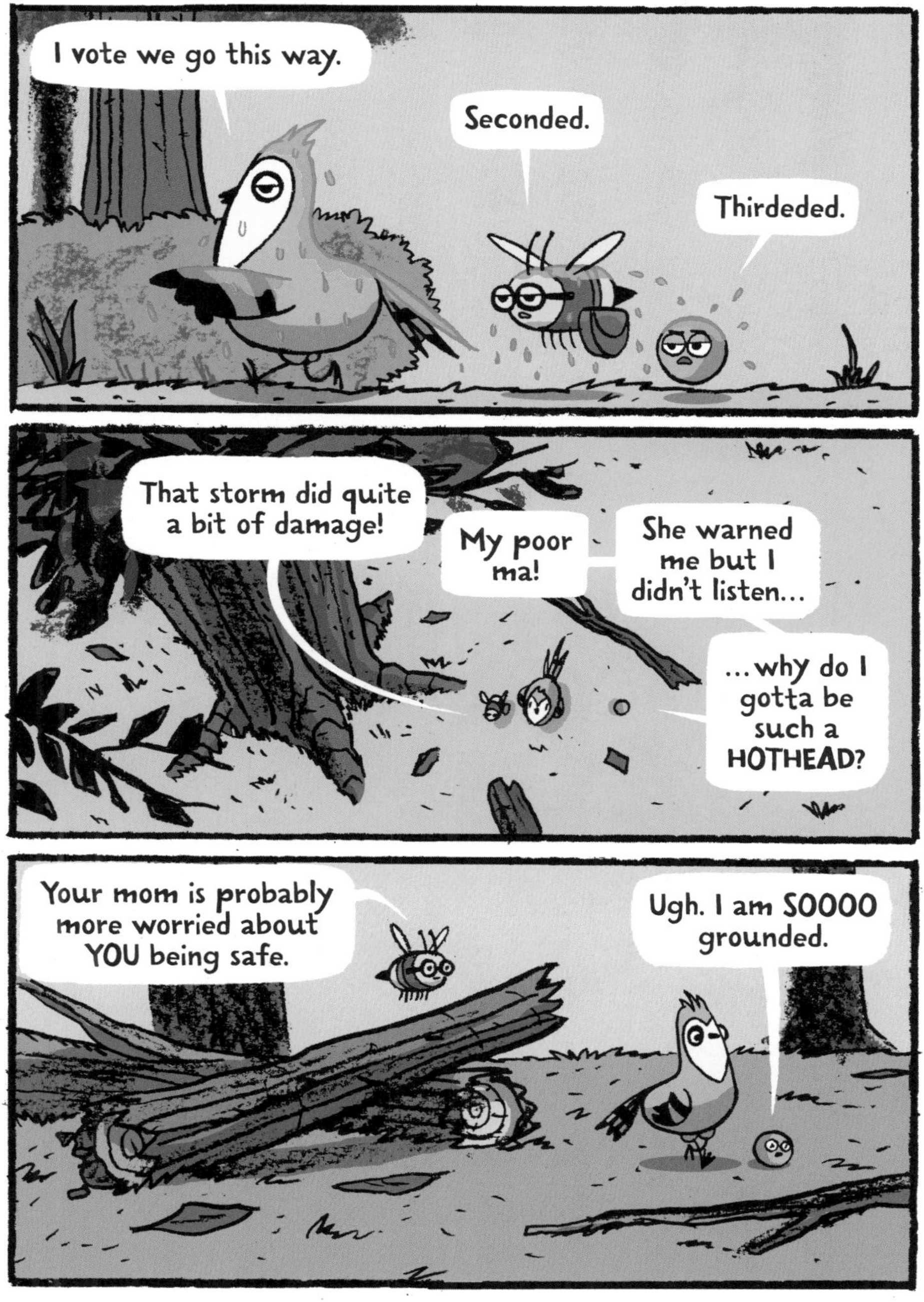
I vote we go this way.
Seconded.
Thirdeded.
That storm did quite a bit of damage!
My poor ma!
She warned me but I didn't listen...
...why do I gotta be such a HOTHEAD?
Your mom is probably more worried about YOU being safe.
Ugh. I am SOOOO grounded.

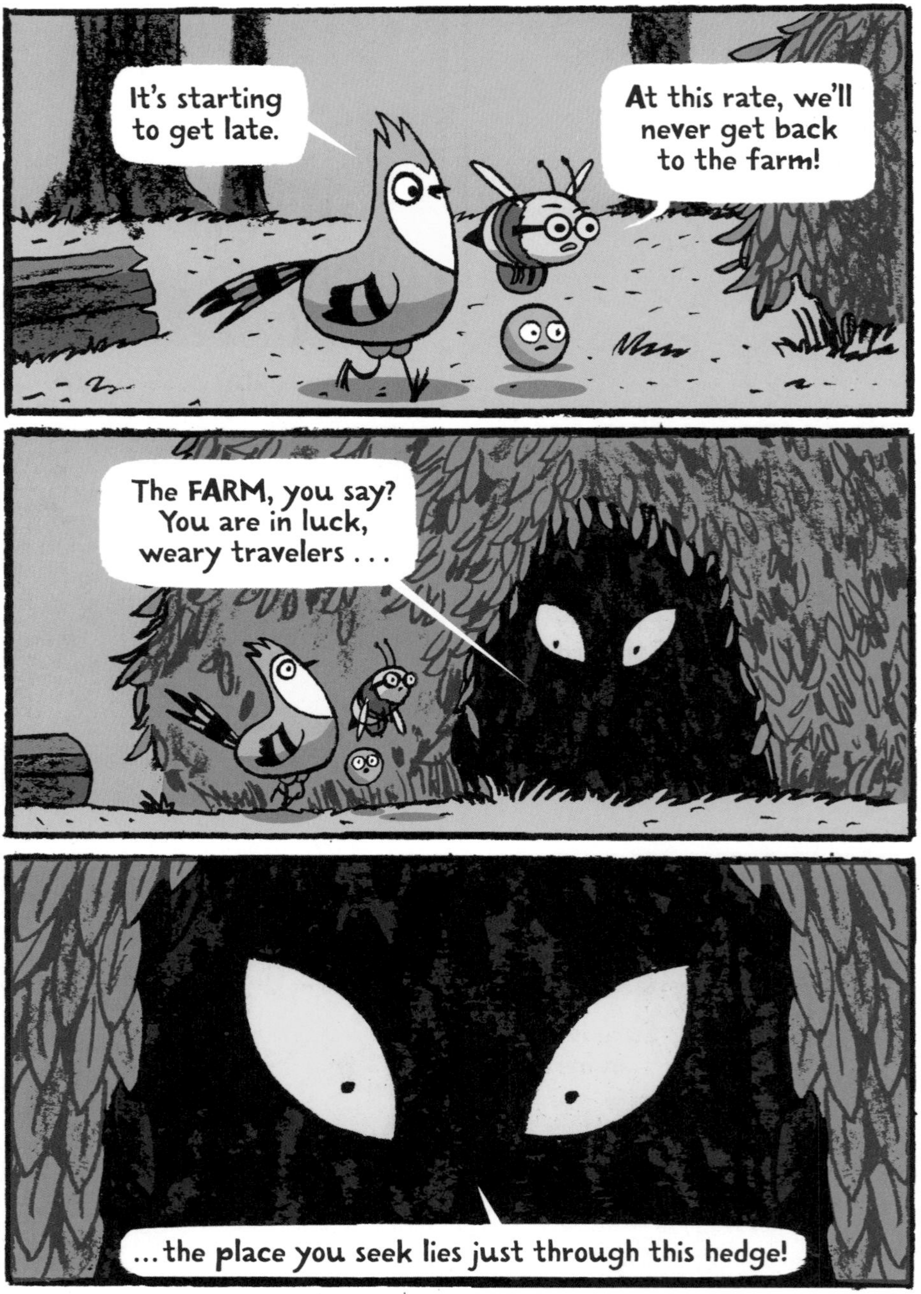
It's starting to get late.
At this rate, we'll never get back to the farm!
The FARM, you say? You are in luck, weary travelers . . .
...the place you seek lies just through this hedge!

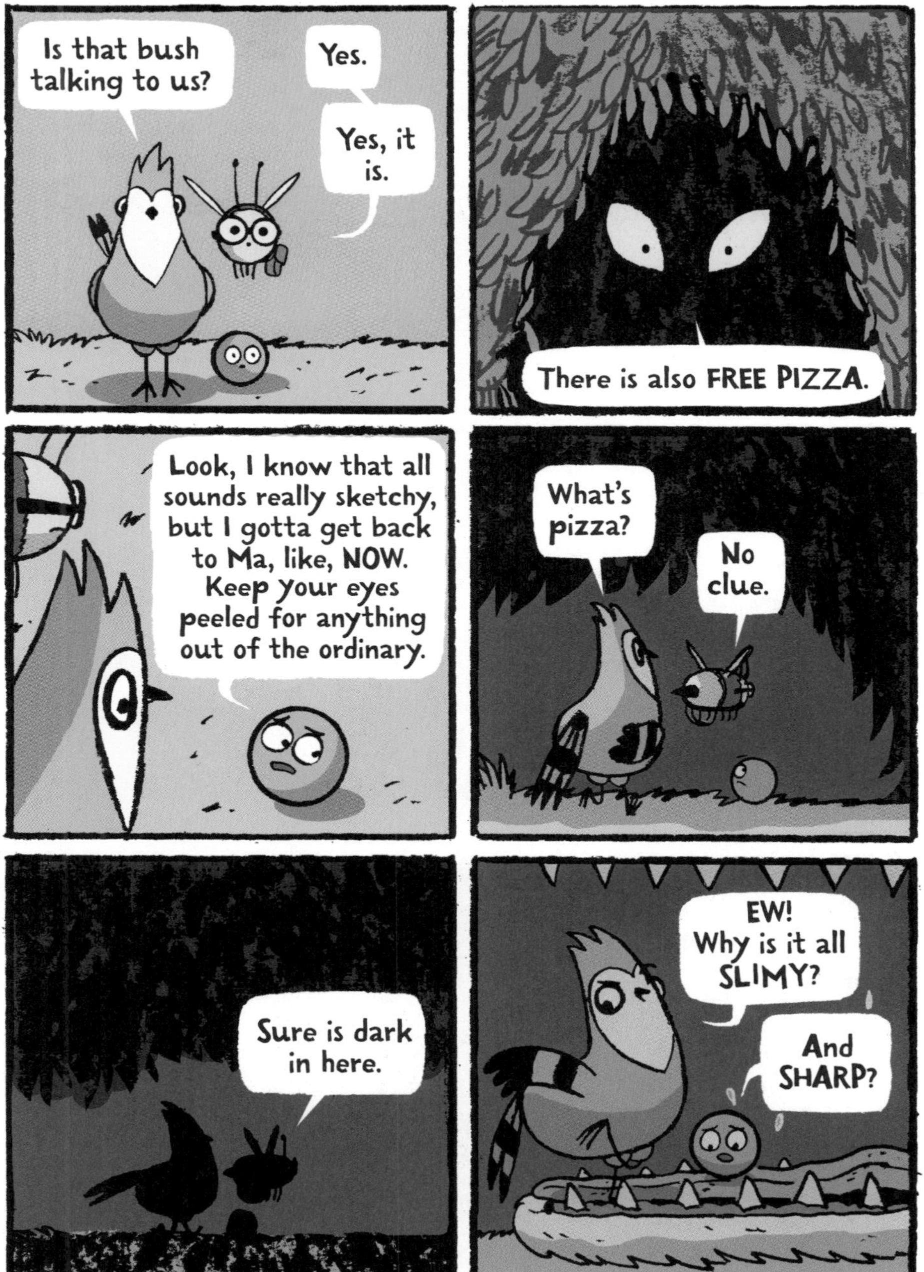
Is that bush talking to us?
Yes.
Yes, it is.
There is also FREE PIZZA.
Look, I know that all sounds really sketchy, but I gotta get back to Ma, like, NOW. Keep your eyes peeled for anything out of the ordinary.
What's pizza?
No clue.
Sure is dark in here.
EW! Why is it all SLIMY?
And SHARP?

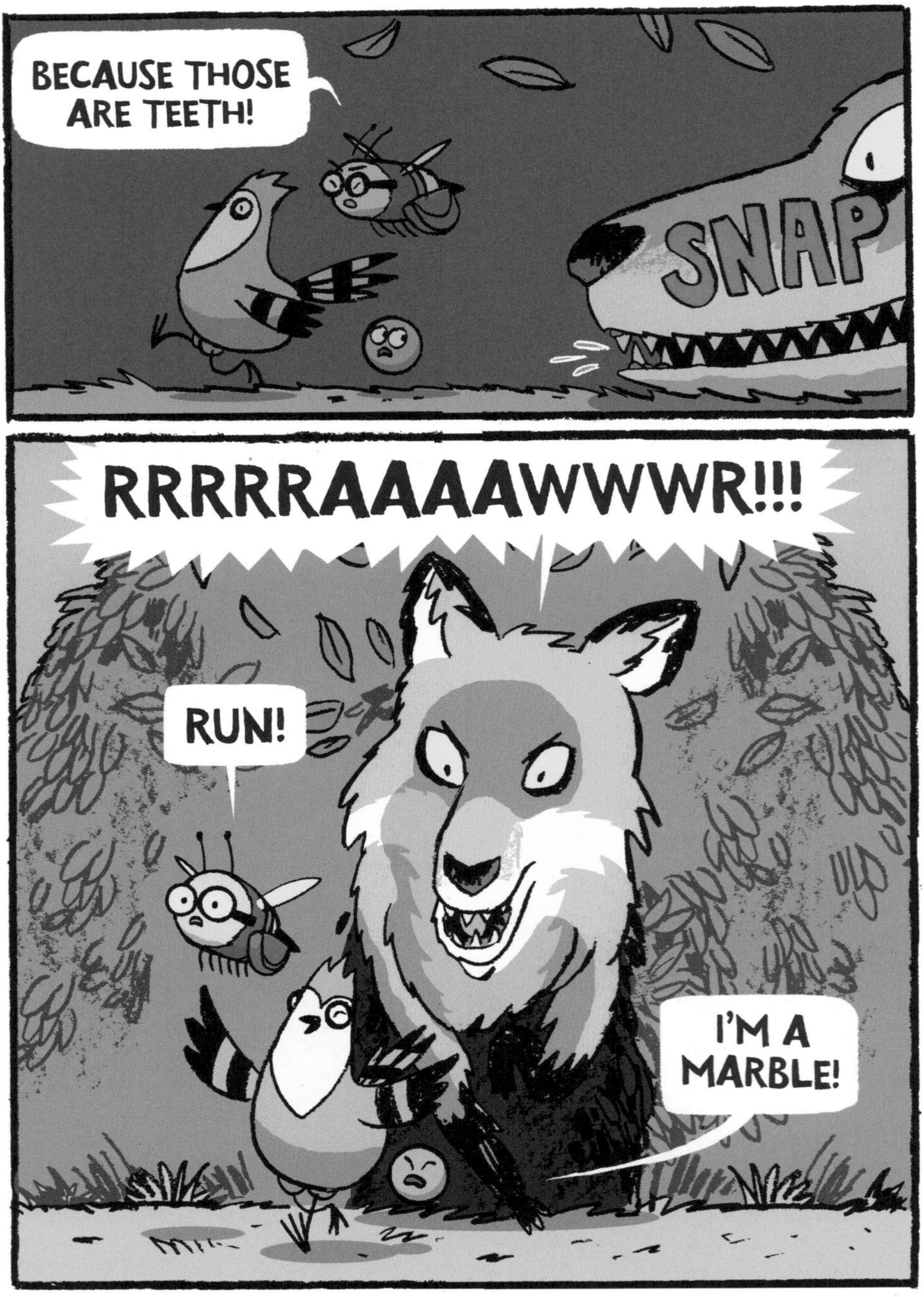
BECAUSE THOSE ARE TEETH!
SNAP
RRRRRAAAAWWWR!!!
RUN!
I'M A MARBLE!

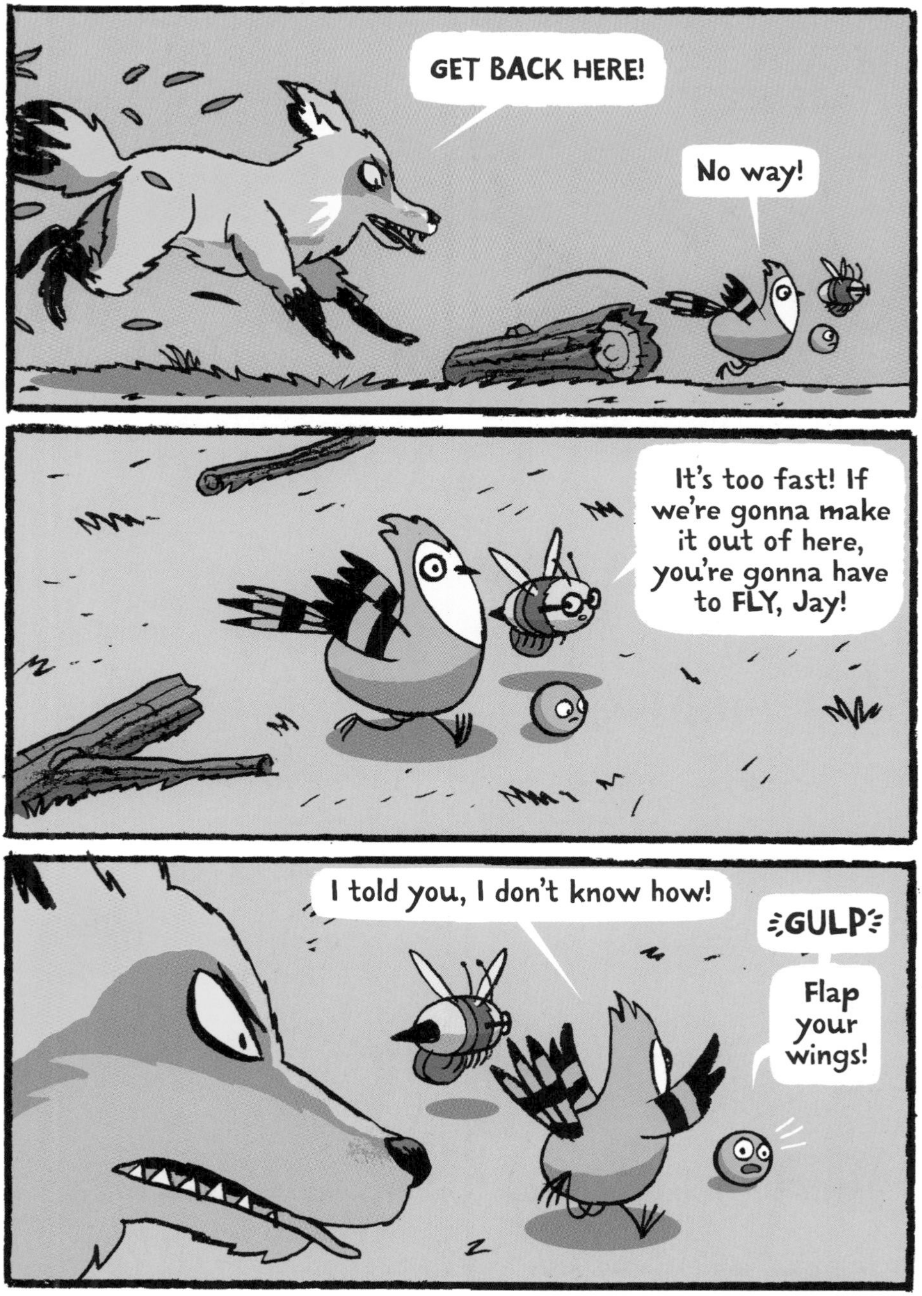
GET BACK HERE!
No way!
It's too fast! If we're gonna make it out of here, you're gonna have to FLY, Jay!
I told you, I don't know how!
GULP
Flap your wings!

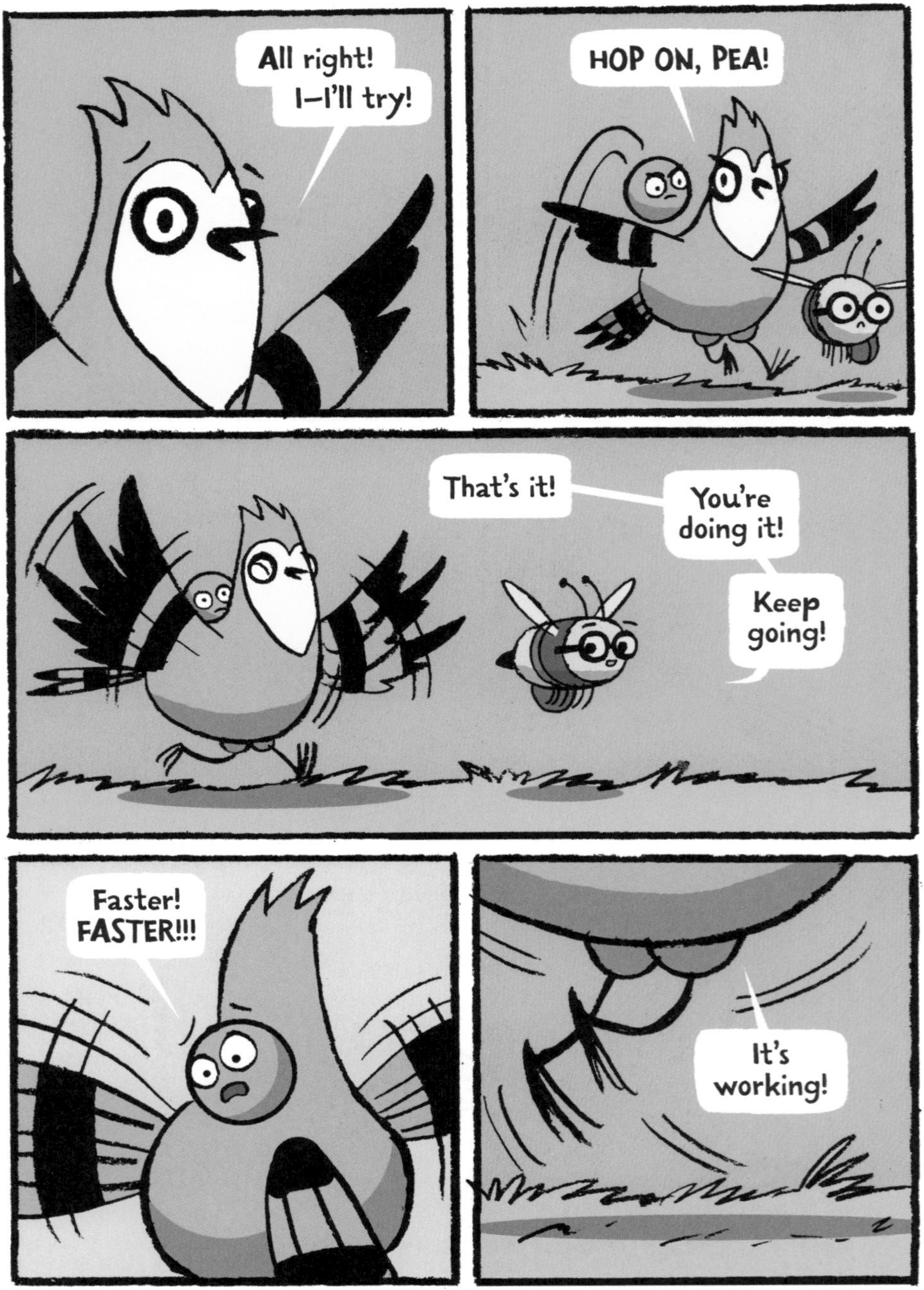
All right! I–I'll try!
HOP ON, PEA!
That's it!
You're doing it!
Keep going!
Faster! FASTER!!!
It's working!

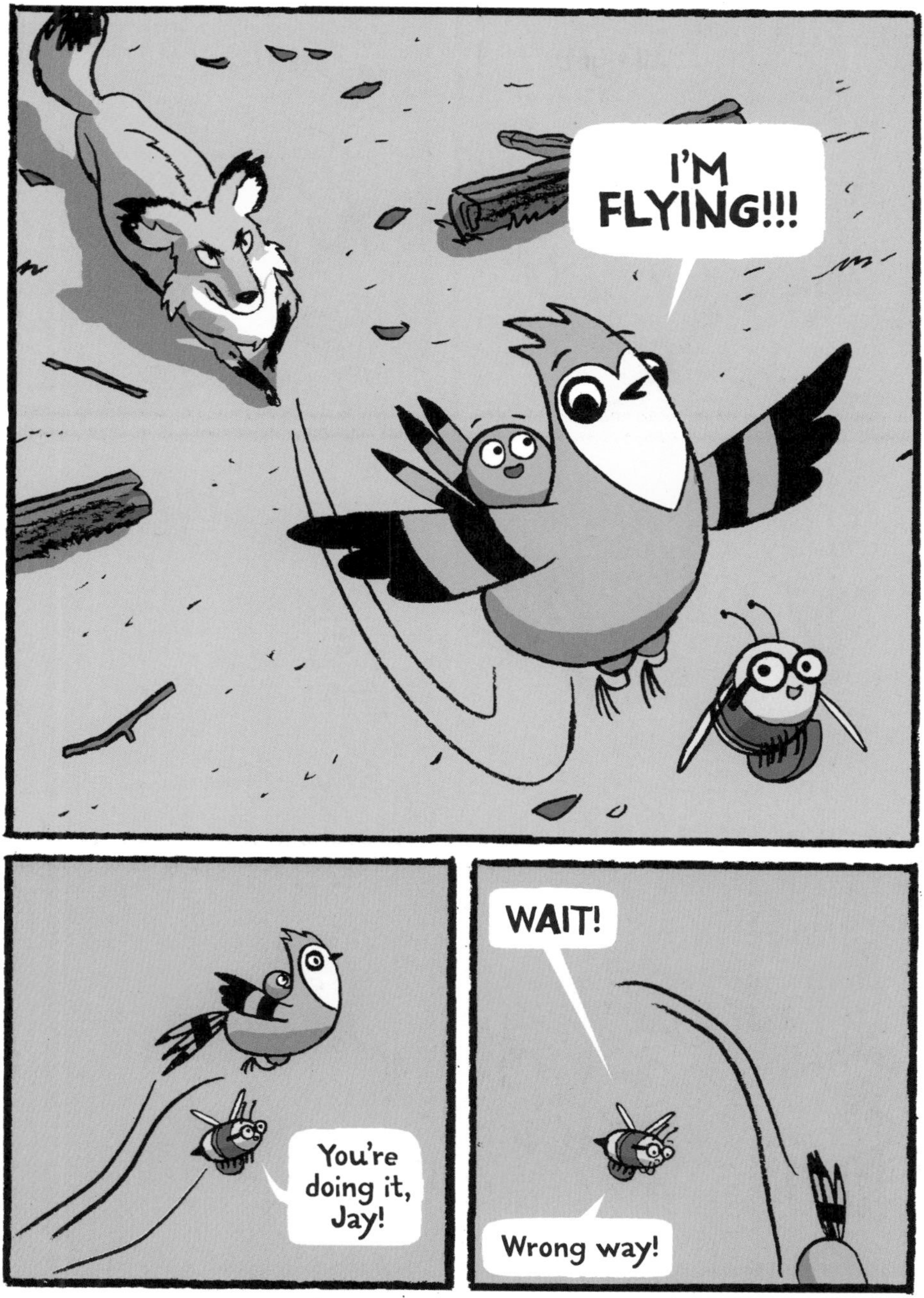
I'M FLYING!!!
You're doing it, Jay!
WAIT!
Wrong way!

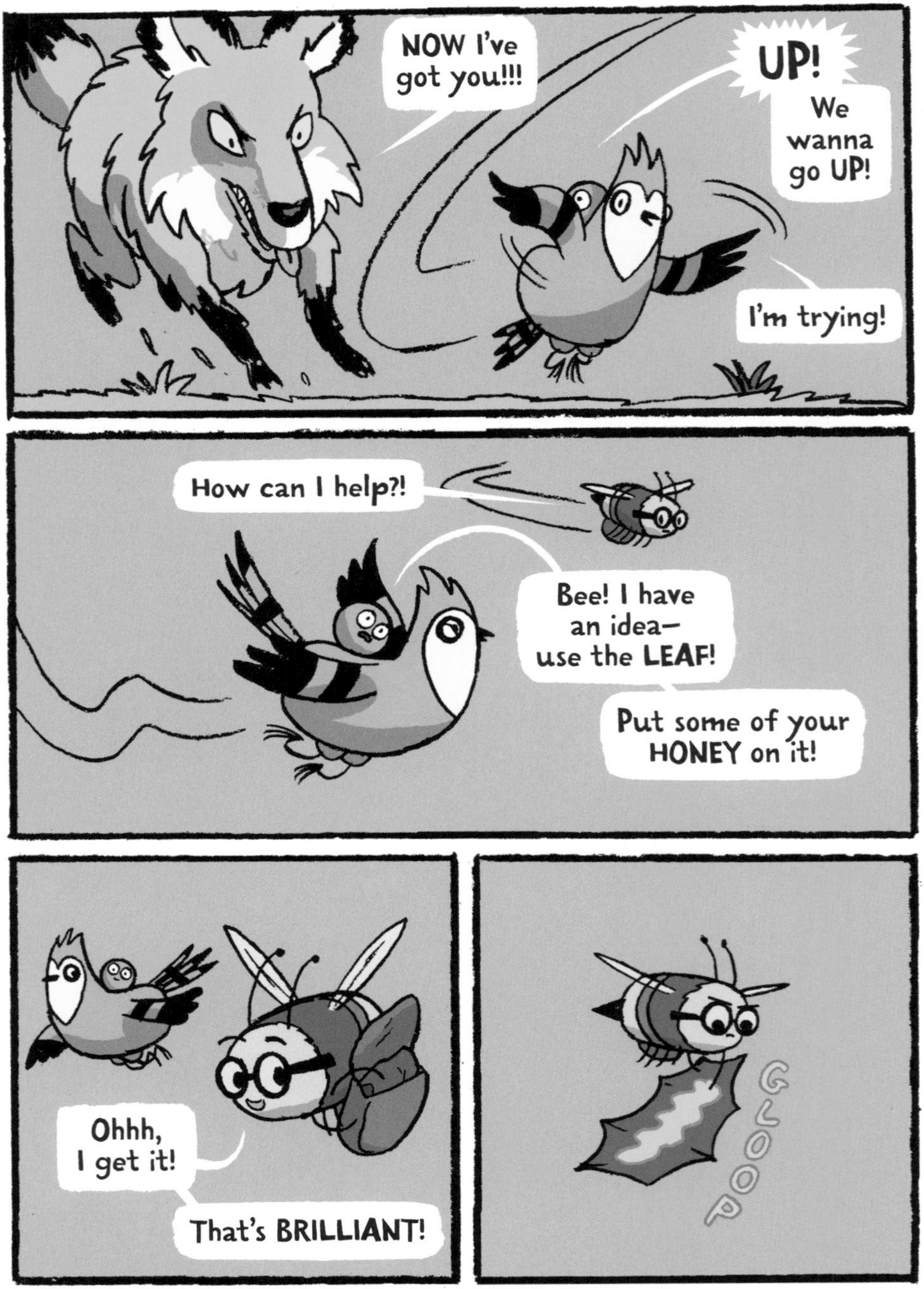
NOW I've got you!!!
UP!
We wanna go UP!
I'm trying!
How can I help?!
Bee! I have an idea— use the LEAF!
Put some of your HONEY on it!
Ohhh, I get it!
That's BRILLIANT!
GLOOP

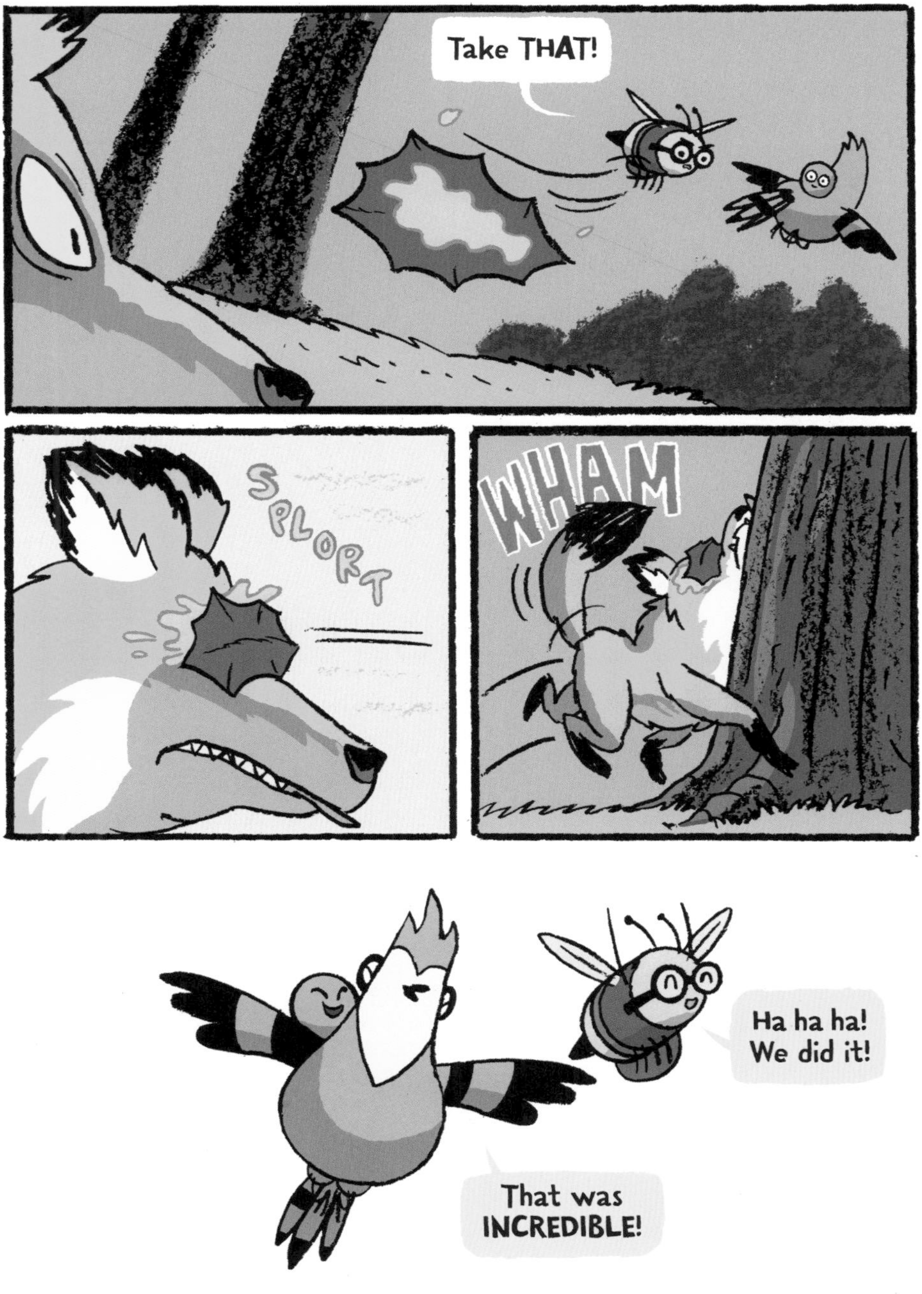
Take THAT!
SPLORT
WHAM
Ha ha ha! We did it!
That was INCREDIBLE!

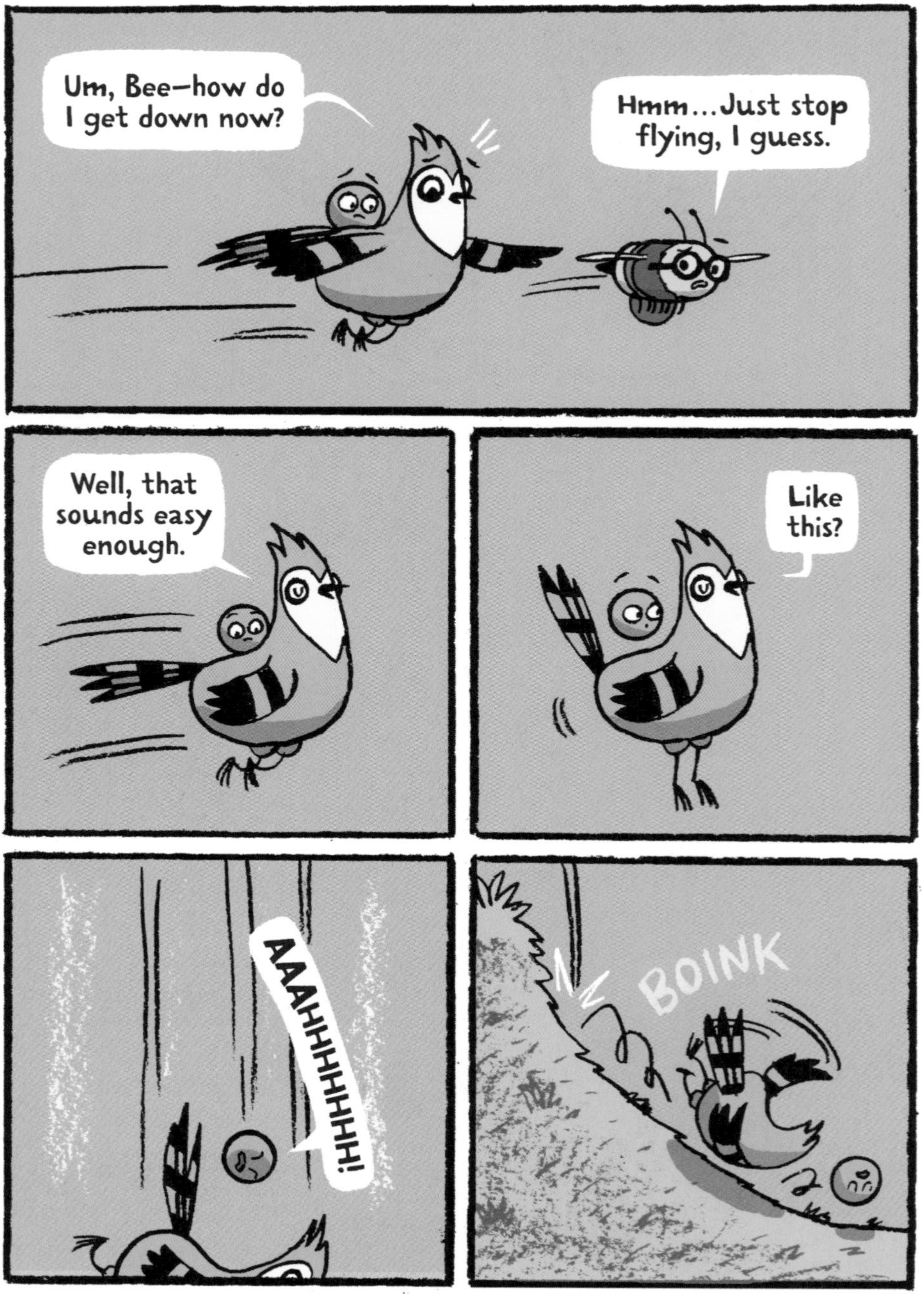

Um, Bee—how do I get down now?
Hmm...Just stop flying, I guess.
Well, that sounds easy enough.
Like this?
AAAHHHHHHH!
BOINK

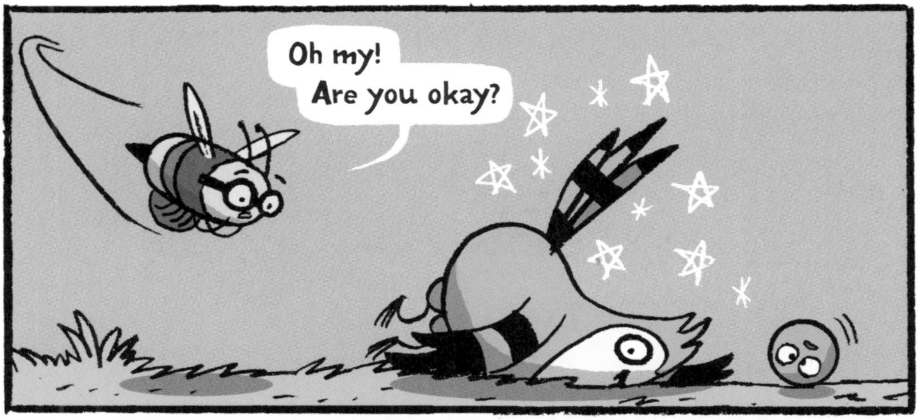
Oh my! Are you okay?

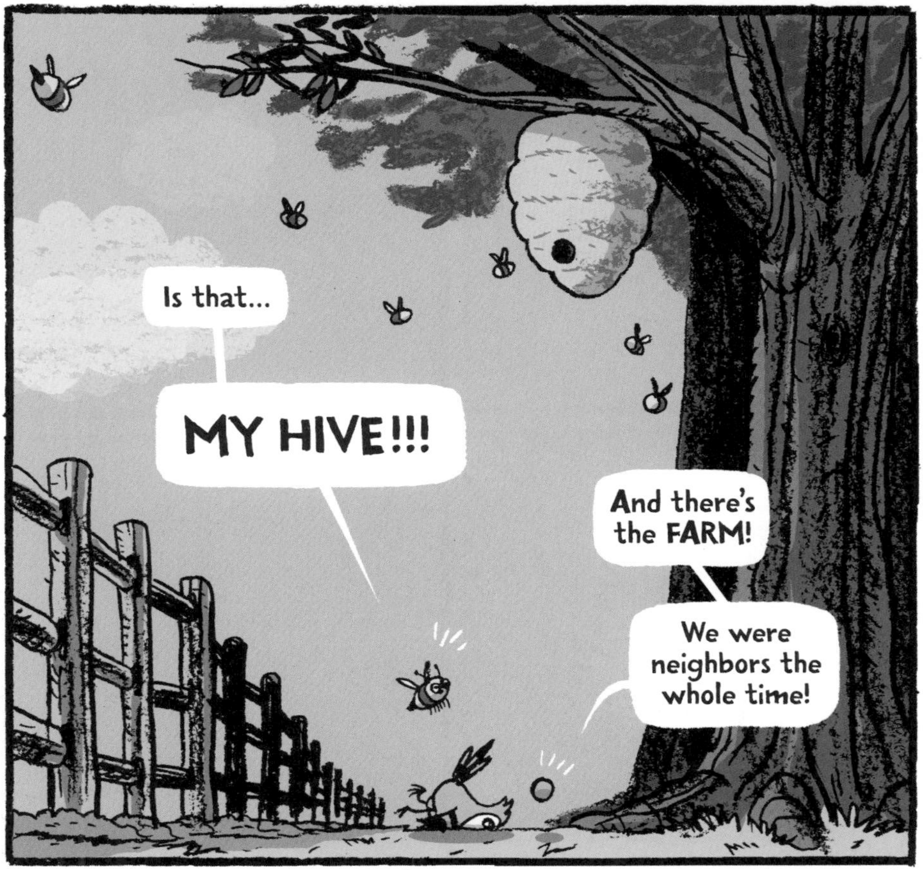
Is that...
MY HIVE!!!
And there's the FARM!
We were neighbors the whole time!

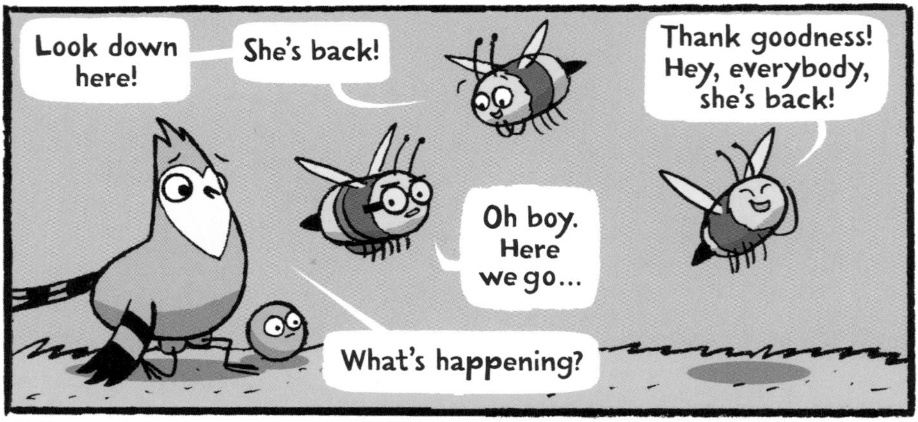
Look down here!
She's back!
Thank goodness! Hey, everybody, she's back!
Oh boy. Here we go...
What's happening?

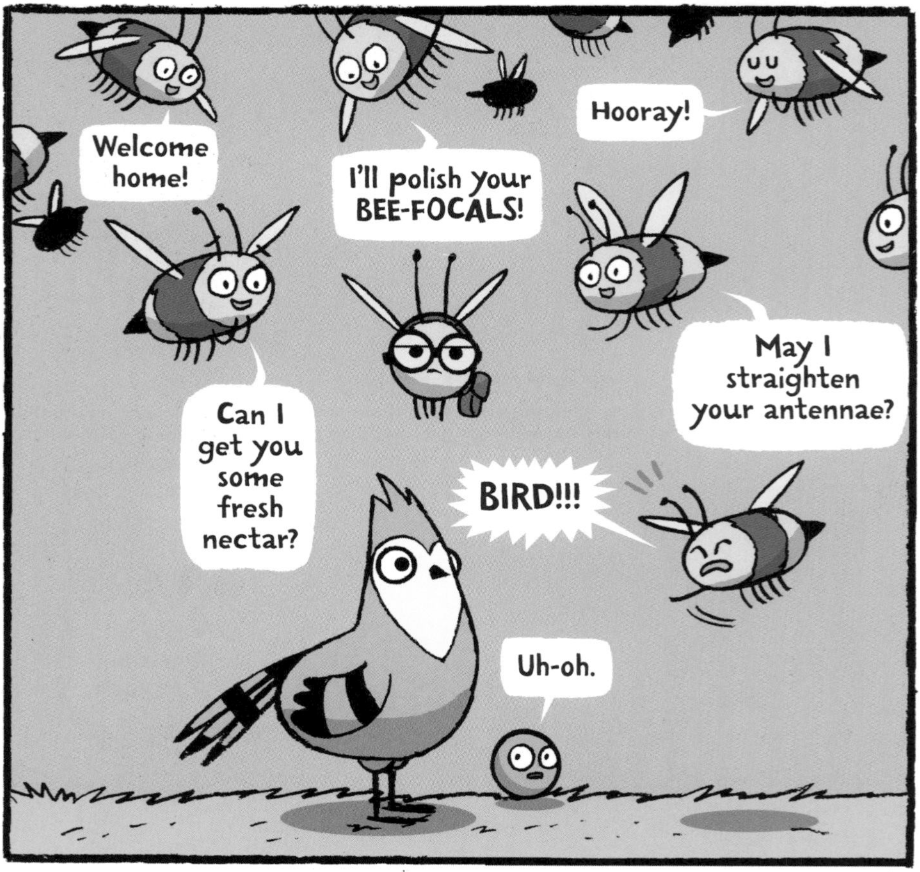
Welcome home!
I'll polish your BEE-FOCALS!
Hooray!
May I straighten your antennae?
Can I get you some fresh nectar?
BIRD!!!
Uh-oh.

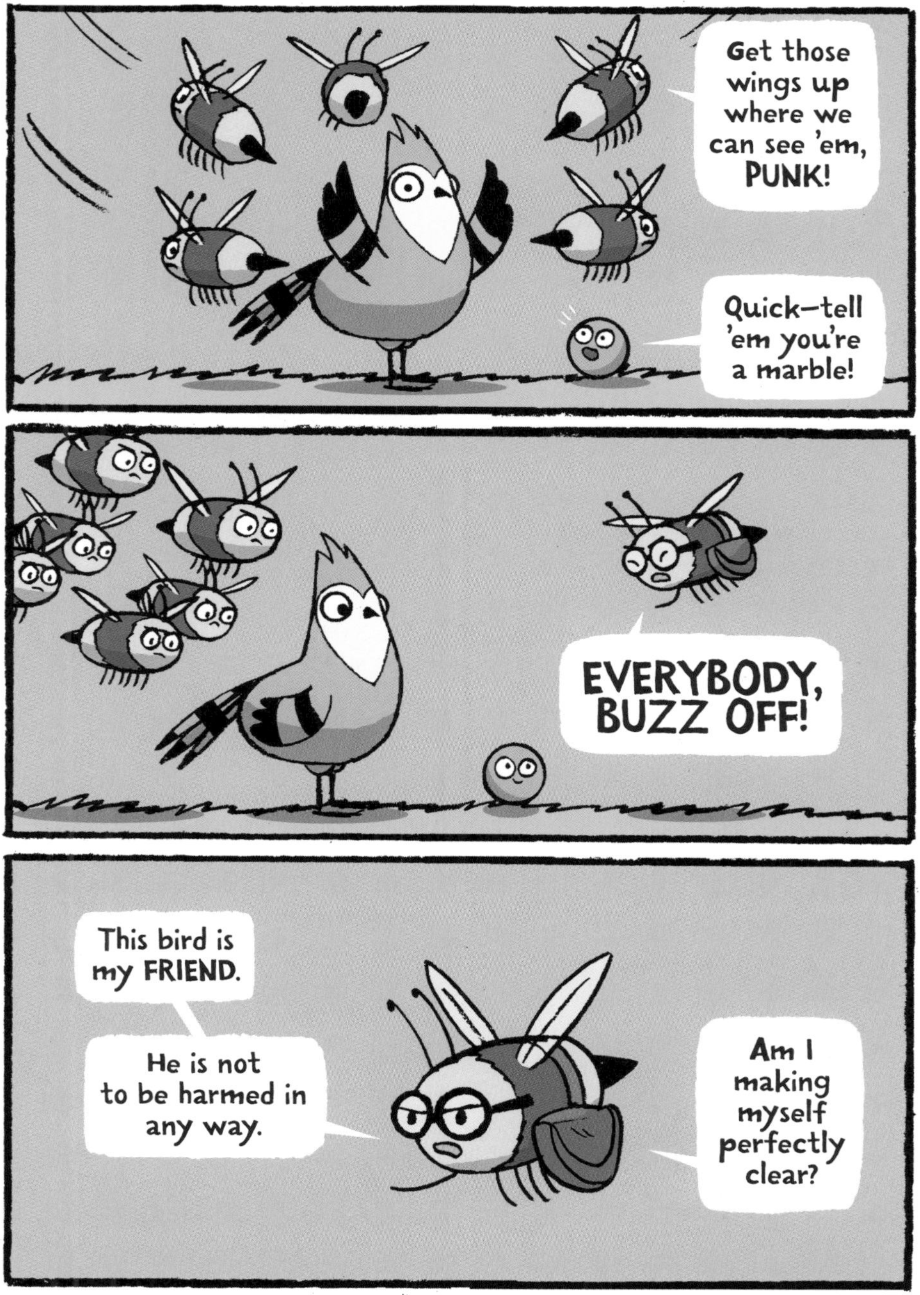

Get those wings up where we can see 'em, PUNK!
Quick—tell 'em you're a marble!
EVERYBODY, BUZZ OFF!
This bird is my FRIEND.
He is not to be harmed in any way.
Am I making myself perfectly clear?

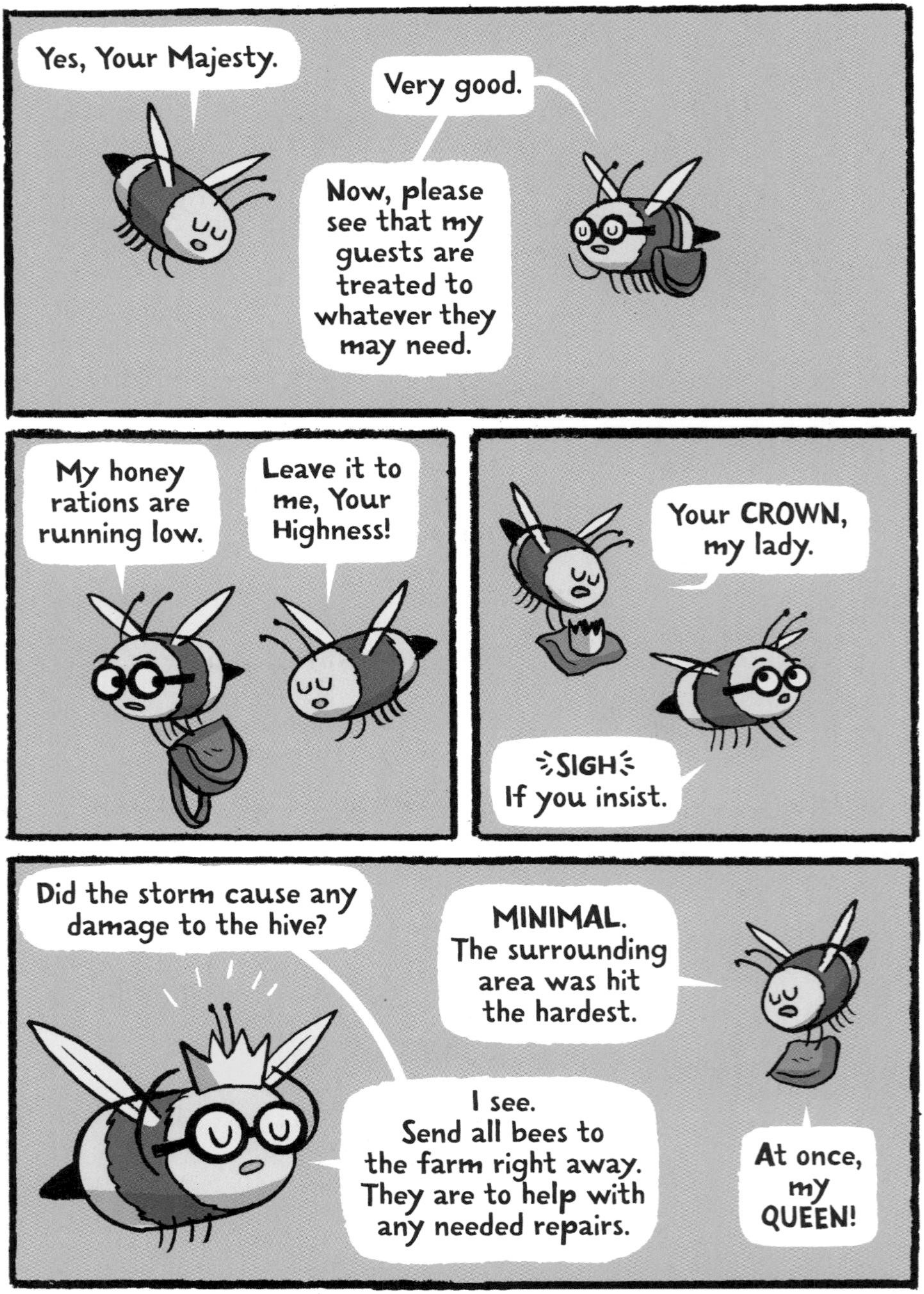
Yes, Your Majesty.
Very good.
Now, please see that my guests are treated to whatever they may need.
My honey rations are running low.
Leave it to me, Your Highness!
Your CROWN, my lady.
SIGH
If you insist.
Did the storm cause any damage to the hive?
MINIMAL. The surrounding area was hit the hardest.
I see. Send all bees to the farm right away. They are to help with any needed repairs.
At once, my QUEEN!

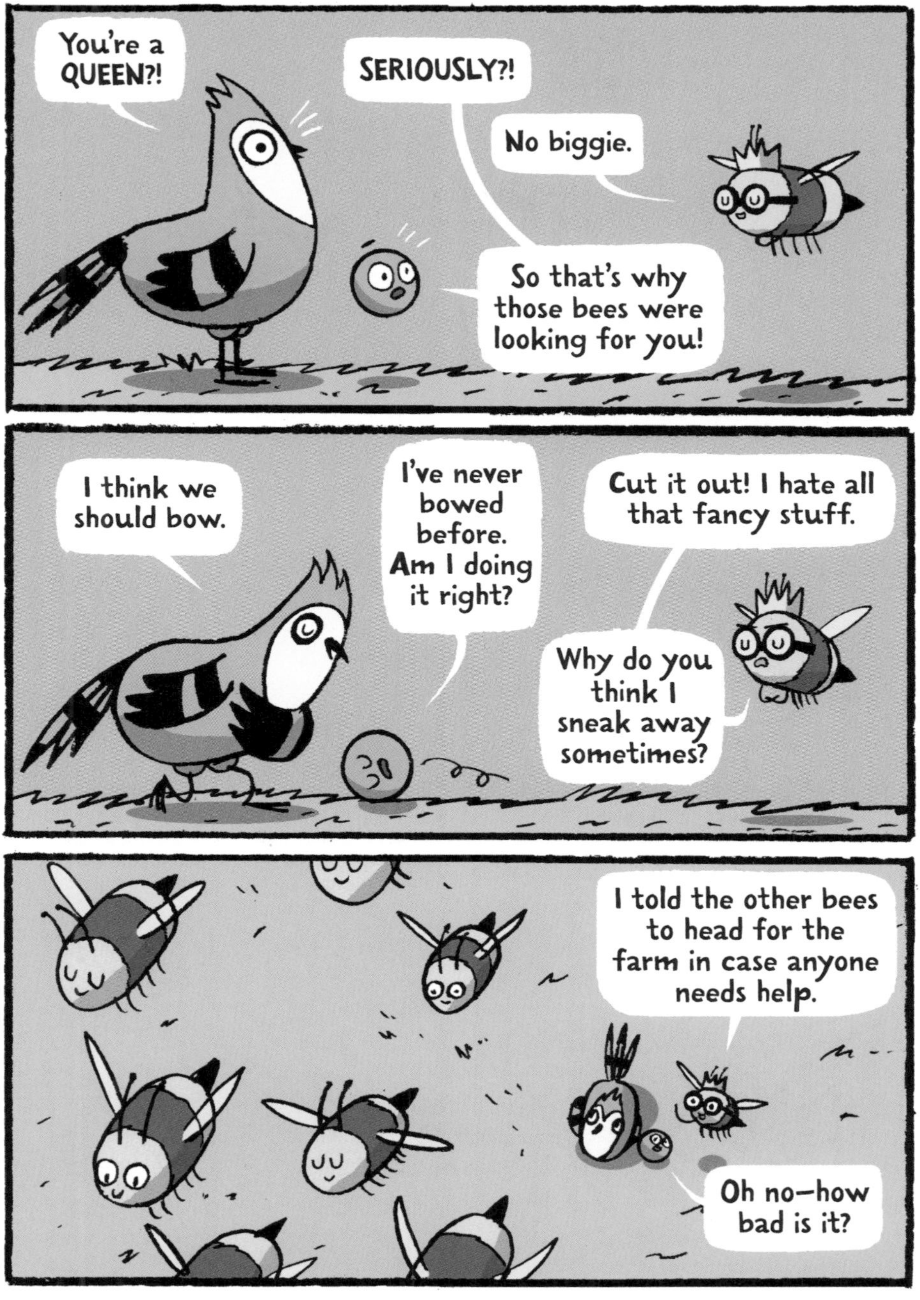
You're a QUEEN?!
SERIOUSLY?!
No biggie.
So that's why those bees were looking for you!
I think we should bow.
I've never bowed before. Am I doing it right?
Cut it out! I hate all that fancy stuff.
Why do you think I sneak away sometimes?
I told the other bees to head for the farm in case anyone needs help.
Oh no—how bad is it?

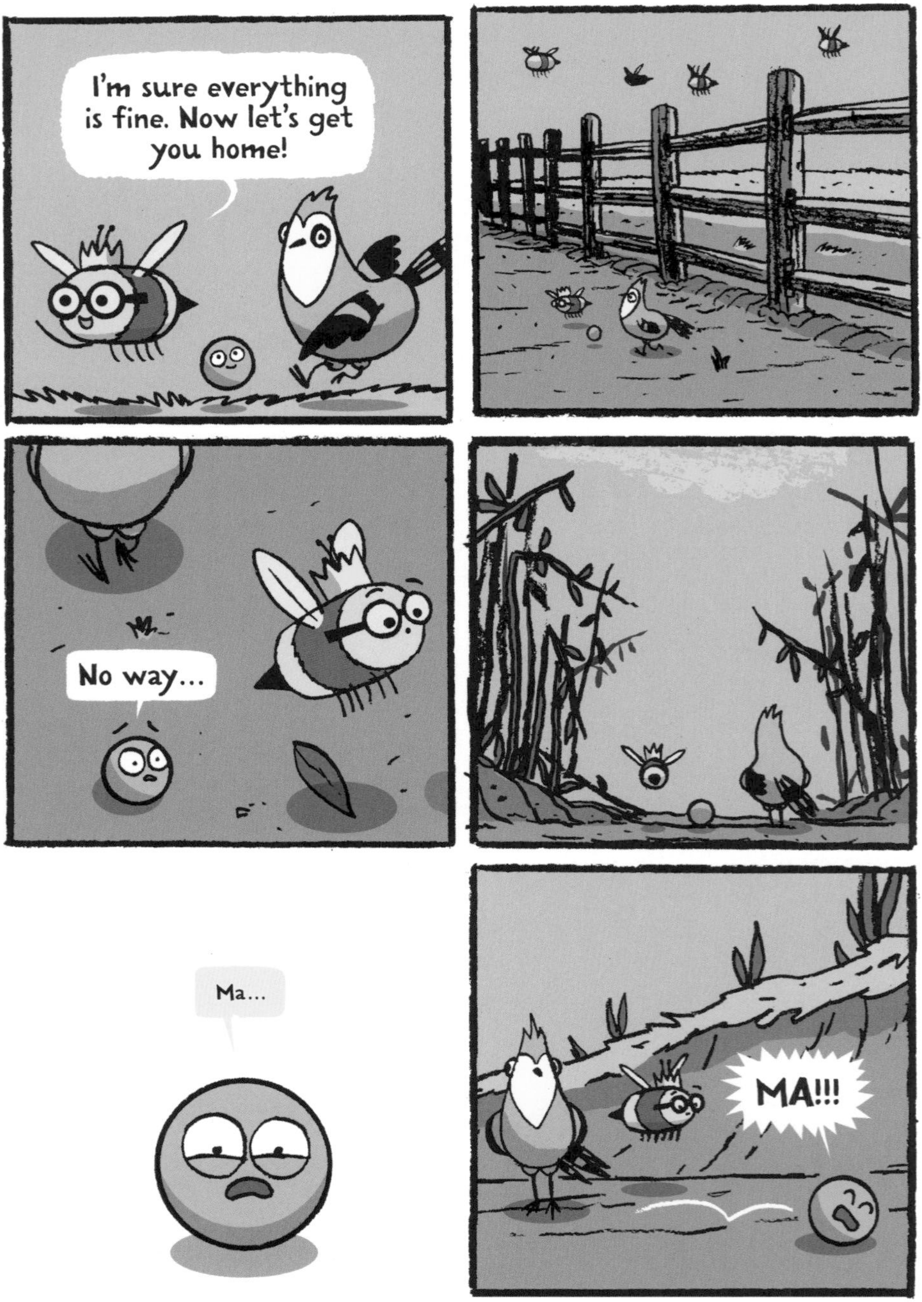
I'm sure everything is fine. Now let's get you home!
No way...
Ma...
MA!!!

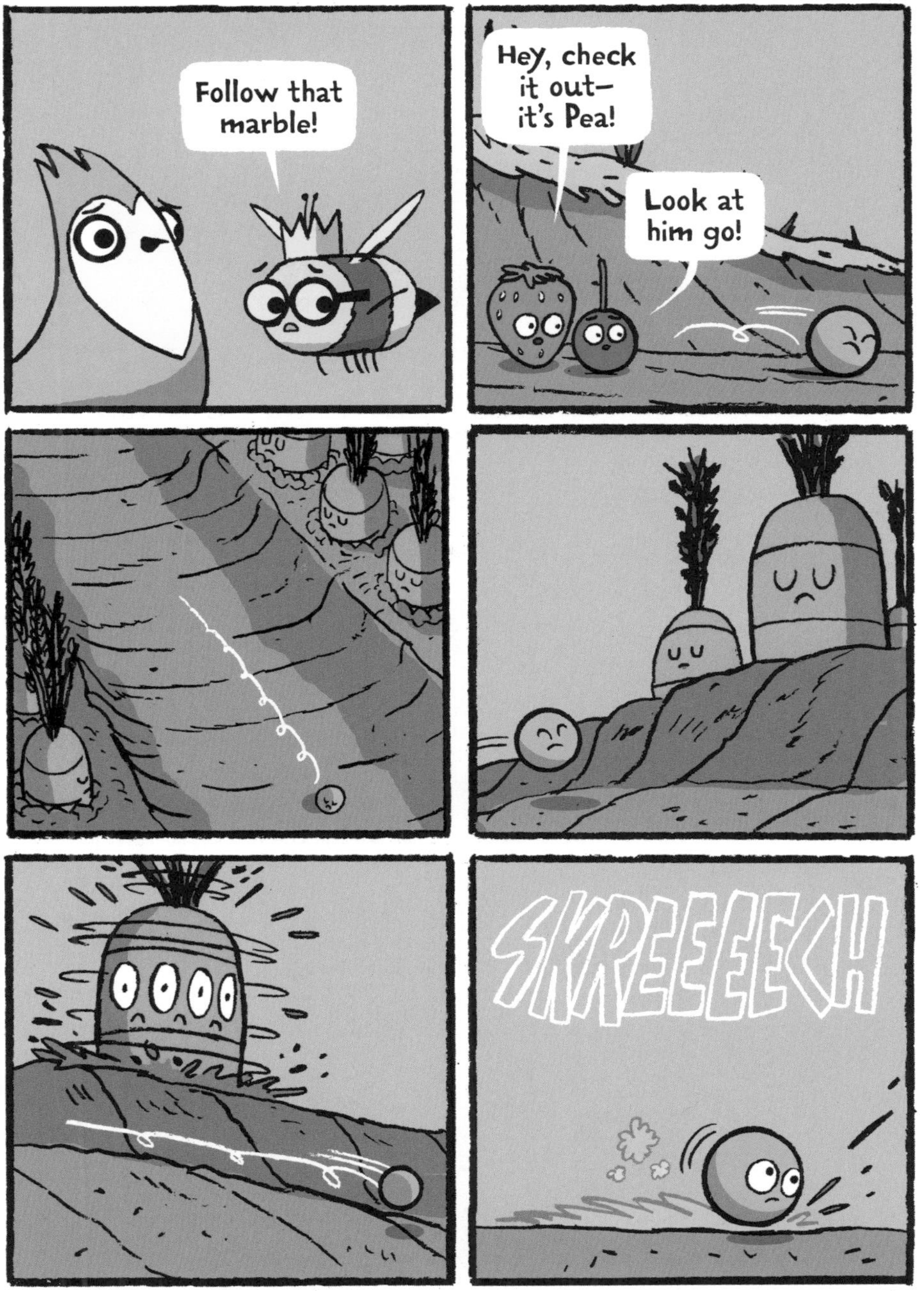
Follow that marble!
Hey, check it out— it's Pea!
Look at him go!
SKREEEEECH

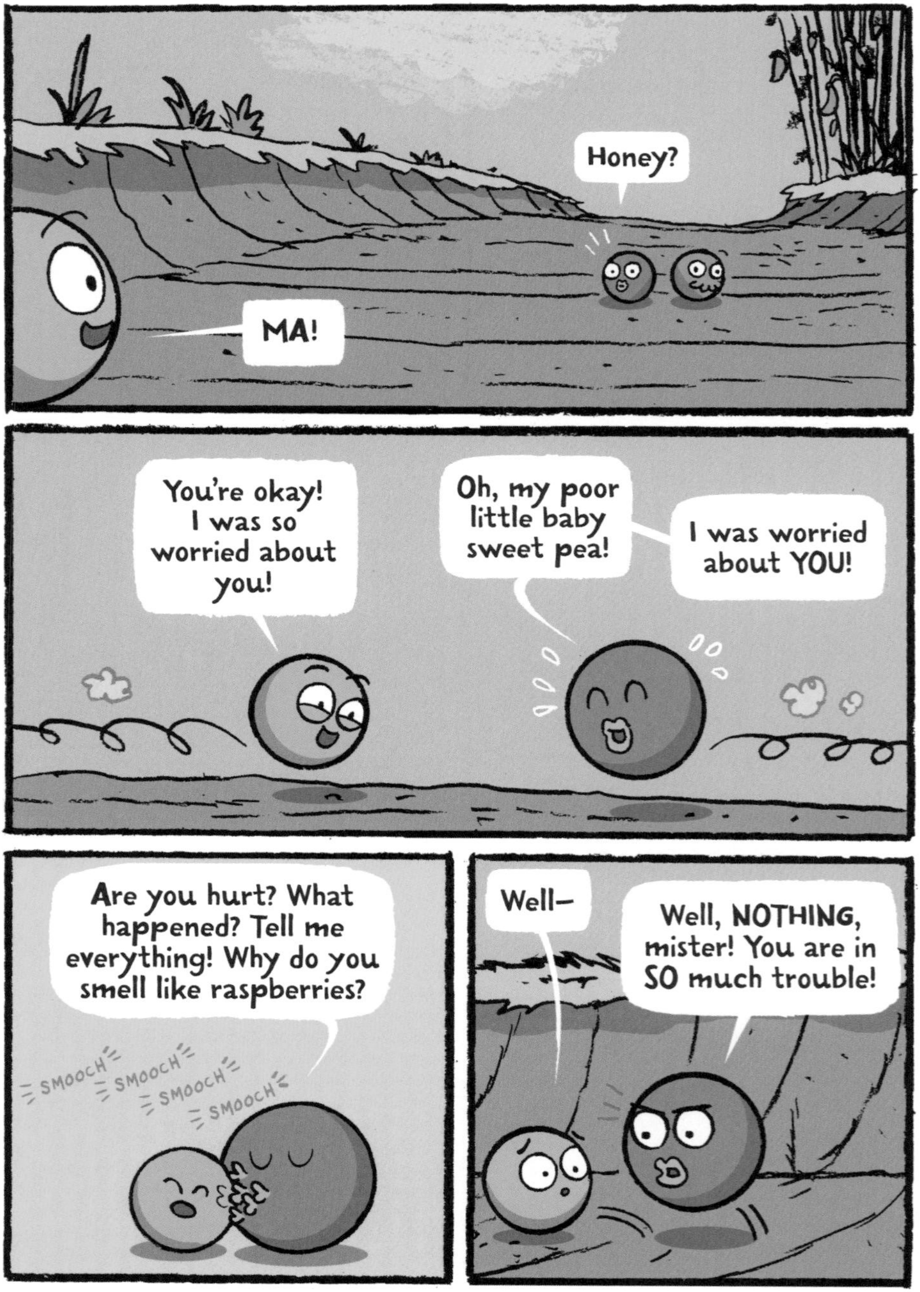
Honey?
MA!
You're okay! I was so worried about you!
Oh, my poor little baby sweet pea!
I was worried about YOU!
Are you hurt? What happened? Tell me everything! Why do you smell like raspberries?
SMOOCH SMOOCH SMOOCH SMOOCH
Well—
Well, NOTHING, mister! You are in SO much trouble!

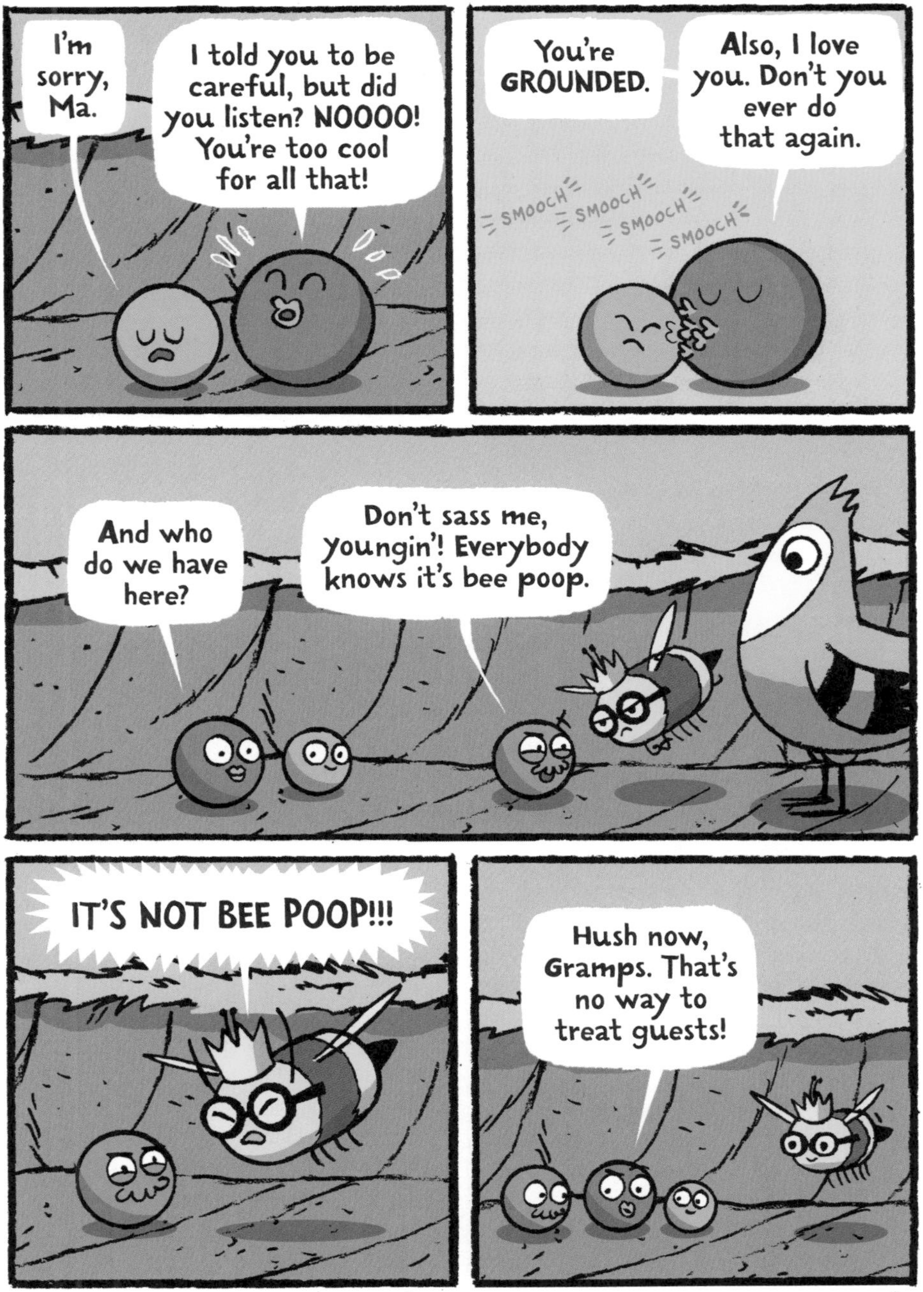
I'm sorry, Ma.
I told you to be careful, but did you listen? NOOOO! You're too cool for all that!
You're GROUNDED.
Also, I love you. Don't you ever do that again.
SMOOCH SMOOCH SMOOCH SMOOCH
And who do we have here?
Don't sass me, youngin'! Everybody knows it's bee poop.
IT'S NOT BEE POOP!!!
Hush now, Gramps. That's no way to treat guests!

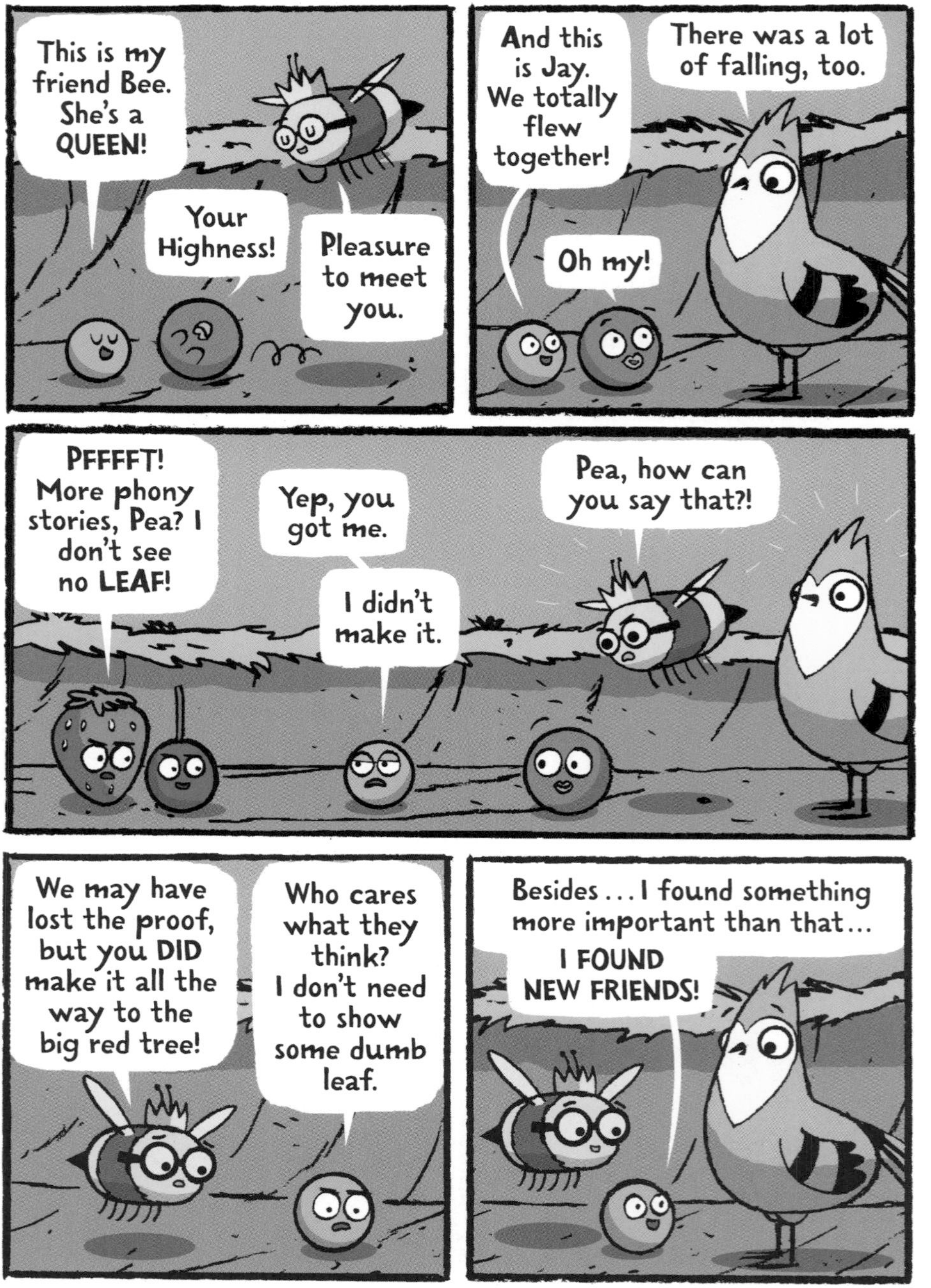
This is my friend Bee. She's a QUEEN!
Your Highness!
Pleasure to meet you.
And this is Jay. We totally flew together!
There was a lot of falling, too.
Oh my!
PFFFFT! More phony stories, Pea? I don't see no LEAF!
Yep, you got me.
I didn't make it.
Pea, how can you say that?!
We may have lost the proof, but you DID make it all the way to the big red tree!
Who cares what they think? I don't need to show some dumb leaf.
Besides . . . I found something more important than that . . .
I FOUND NEW FRIENDS!

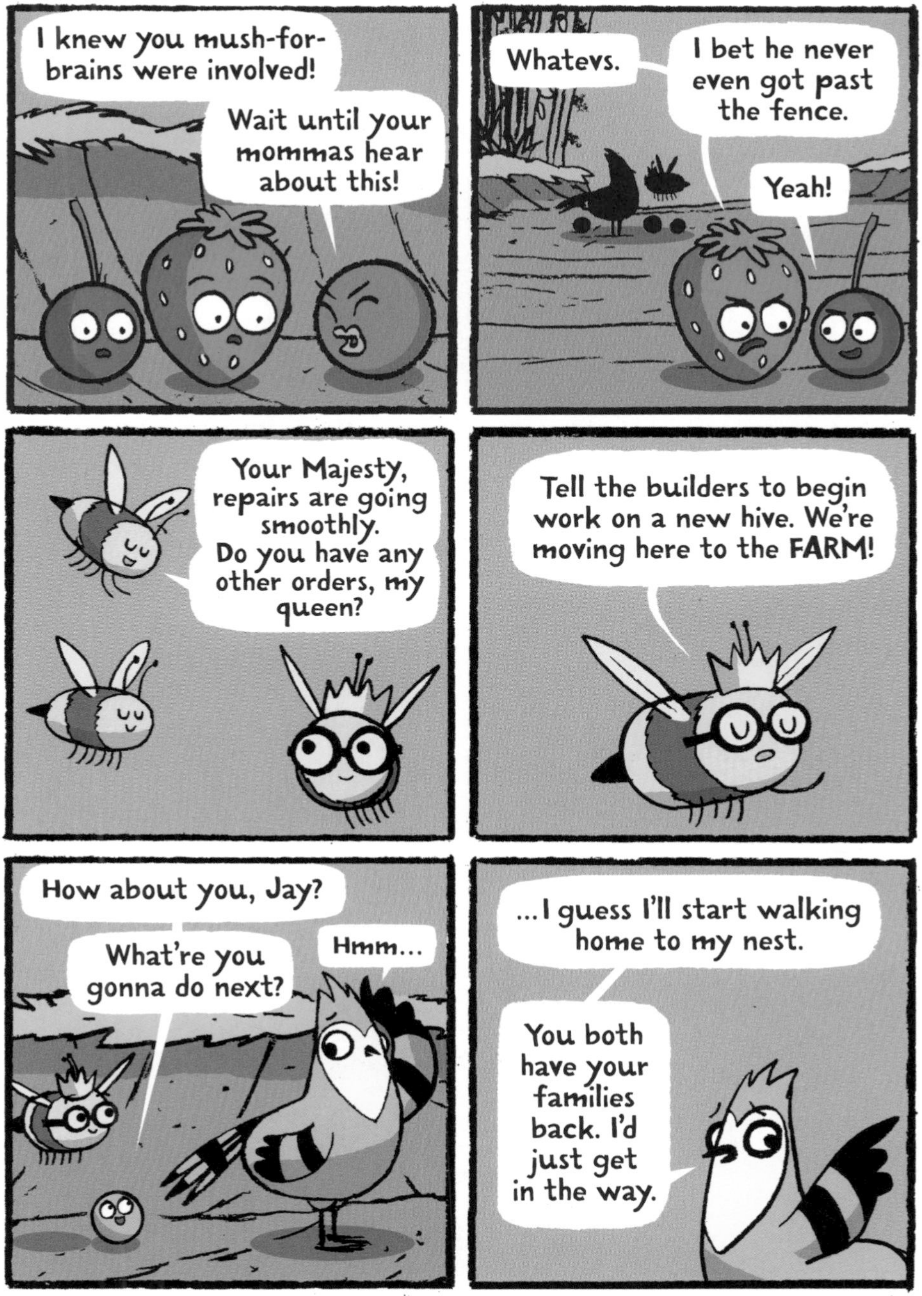
I knew you mush-for-brains were involved!
Wait until your mommas hear about this!
Whatevs.
I bet he never even got past the fence.
Yeah!
Your Majesty, repairs are going smoothly. Do you have any other orders, my queen?
Tell the builders to begin work on a new hive. We're moving here to the FARM!
How about you, Jay?
What're you gonna do next?
Hmm...
...I guess I'll start walking home to my nest.
You both have your families back. I'd just get in the way.

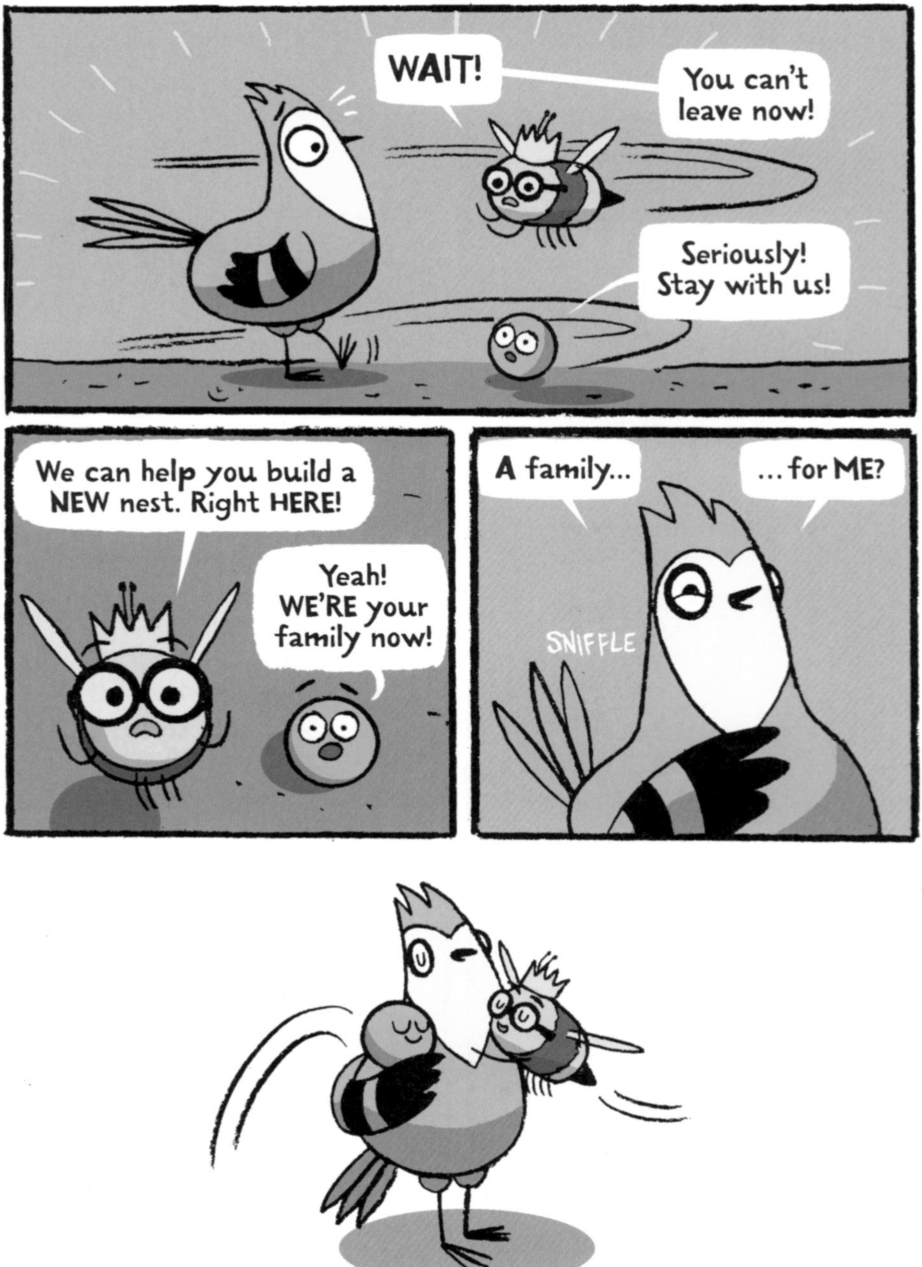
WAIT!
You can't leave now!
Seriously! Stay with us!
We can help you build a NEW nest. Right HERE!
Yeah! WE'RE your family now!
A family...
... for ME?
SNIFFLE

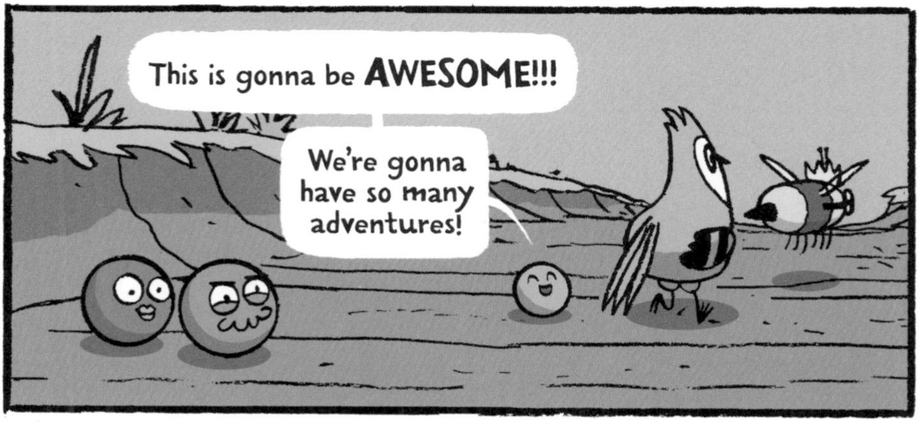
This is gonna be AWESOME!!!
We're gonna have so many adventures!

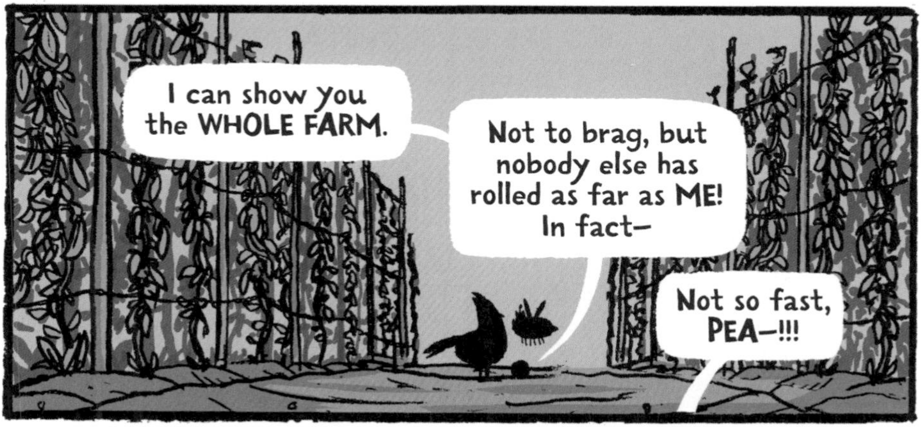
I can show you the WHOLE FARM.
Not to brag, but nobody else has rolled as far as ME! In fact–
Not so fast, PEA–!!!

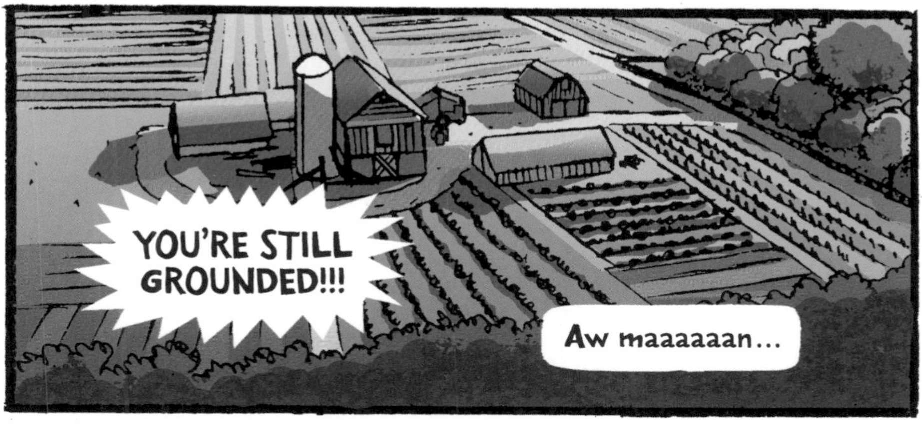
YOU'RE STILL GROUNDED!!!
Aw maaaaaan...

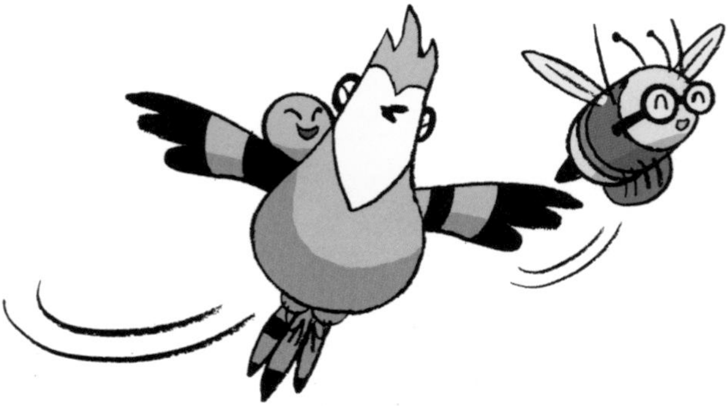

Thank you to Bret Parks, Juliet Parks, Elise Parks, Robin Parks, and Ssalefish Comics, without whom this book would not have been possible.

HarperAlley is an imprint of HarperCollins Publishers.

Pea, Bee, & Jay #1: Stuck Together

For information address HarperCollins Children's Books, a division of HarperCollins Publishers, 195 Broadway, New York, NY 10007.
www.harperalley.com

Library of Congress Control Number: 2019953352
ISBN 978-0-06-298117-2 – ISBN 978-0-06-298116-5 (pbk.)

The artist used pencils, paper, a computer, and bee poop (lots and lots of bee poop) to create the digital illustrations for this book.
Typography by Erica De Chavez and Andrew Arnold
20 21 22 23 24 GPS 10 9 8 7 6 5 4 3
❖
First Edition